ROXIE'S ALIEN KING

DEDICATION

To the readers who like their spice a little primal.

BOOK - MA

This book is intended for mature audiences for adult language, sexual content, and violence. It deals with themes of PTSD, hostile environments, gun use, gun violence, and primal kink.

VÒLLﬃÃIﬃﬁ GLOSSARY

RŮṢAD'Ù – A BONDING CEREMONY, OFTEN CONSISTENT WITH LOCAL TRADITION.

ZHUSHE – AN UNMATED FEMALE VOLLO WHO IS OF AGE

VÒLLØ – THE NATIVE PEOPLE OF SHOJO, THIS WORD IS USED LIKE HUMAN.

PEHOLOE – ELDERS WHO HAVE LOVED AND LOST THEIR ĜHA.

UHICHI – LARGE, CROW-LIKE MOUNTS USED FOR MILITARY FLIGHT.

UR'E GU – A SWEET HONEYED BREAD OFTEN EATEN FOR BREAKFAST OR DESSERT

ĜHA – PARTNER WHO MAKES THE SECOND HEART BEAT, OR A SOULMATE.

ĜHAJO – PLURAL OF ĜHA

JISA – AN ANATOMICAL SHIELD THAT PROTECTS THE SKIN

TSARE – A DRINK SIMILAR TO WINE

D'O GO CHU MERCHU – "MY ENERGY IS YOURS."

ECHENO – A SPICY DISH SERVED TRADITIONALLY IN VALKARRA

KORÒVÒ – A WHALE-LIKE CREATURE THAT MAKES THE SEA LOOK LIKE STARS AND SPEAKS TELEPATHICALLY

CHYAŘÚ – SHRIMP-LIKE CREATURES, OFTEN EATEN BY LARGER SEA ANIMALS

VELAHIPU – A PREPARATORY CELEBRATION THAT INCLUDES A COLLECTION OF TRADITIONS USED TO CELEBRATE AN IMPENDING BONDING CEREMONY.

NGI – A DIMINUTIVE FOR MOTHER. LIKE MOM OR MOMMA.

GHODE – STUPID, DUMB, OR SILLY.

GHONO – JERK.

NUSOSAN LANGUAGE

ẄEYA – MY LOVE.

LIYE – OF THE HEAVENS, OR PARADISE IN THE CURRENT LIFE.

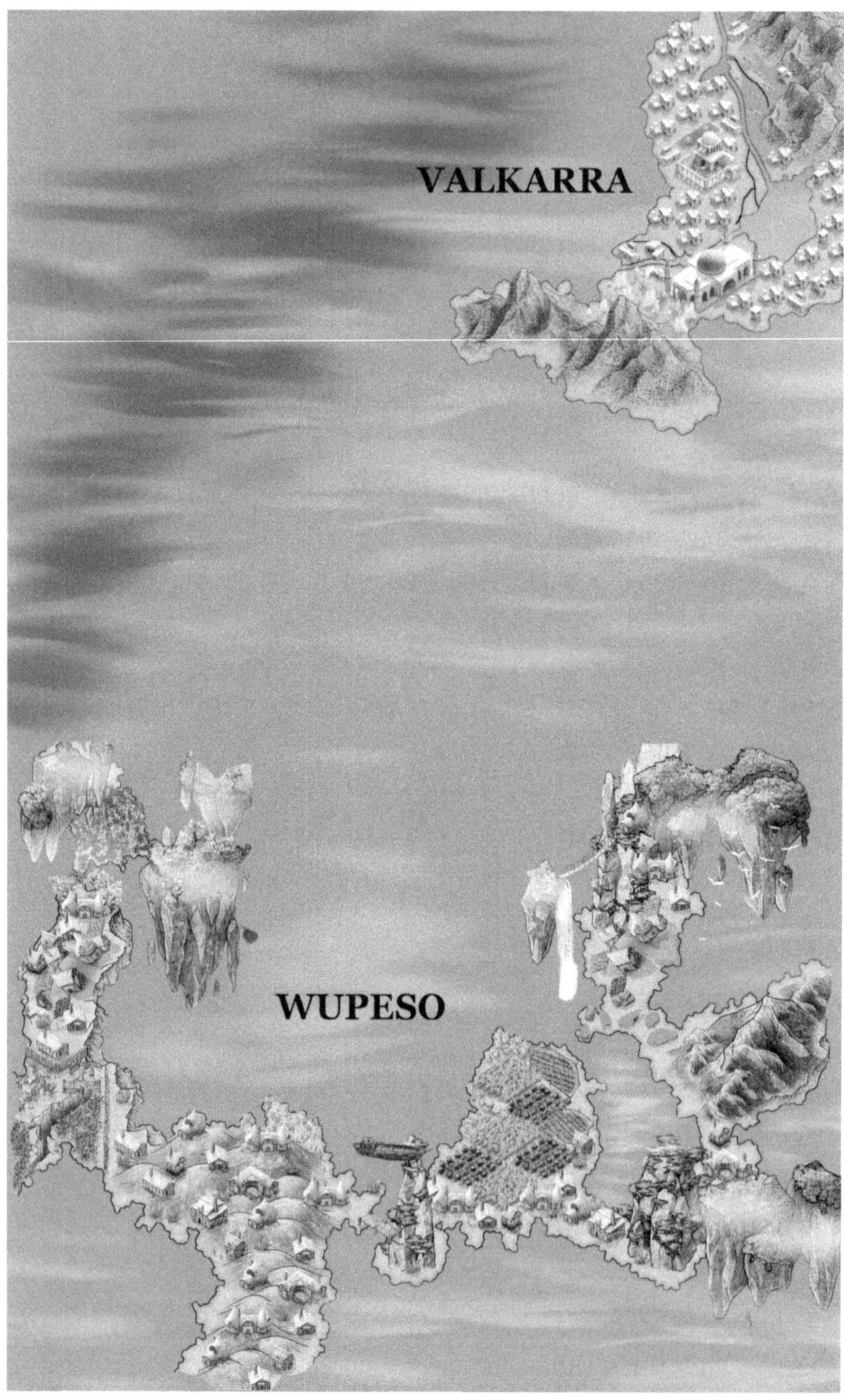
VALKARRA
WUPESO

CHAPTER ONE

Roxie

My skin itches. It's been a month since the *r̈uṣad'ù* ended, and nothing has changed. Vera and Kano are still in their newlywed bubble. Aston still sneaks out every night to fight with Llazho. And I still can't sleep. Instead, I relive the *SS Herculean* every time I close my eyes. I watch my bullets crunch against the monsters' skin, hear the men yell, their skin rend, and smell the metallic scent of blood. When I've had enough of that nightmare, I'll force myself to wake up. I go through the motions, shower, dress, and make my bed before finding my way to the floating island and sitting on the ledge. I'll sit there until the sun rises, join the women for whatever activities we have that day, count my bullets, and go to bed. Rinse and repeat. I've done this for Shojo's version of thirty days, and I was sick of it.

My nails scrape across the raw skin of my forearm. My rash developed three days after Vera and Kano's *r̈uṣad'ù*, and it's only gotten worse. I'd hidden it beneath my clothes for the most part, but Aston saw it one night when we both snuck out of the loft and demanded I ask Blossom about it. Blossom, the peach she is, scanned it with her fancy tech and unhelpfully determined it was either an allergy, a side-effect of the radiation, a reaction to stress, or some combination of the three. She recommended asking the healer, Zhalisee, for some healing salve and keeping my skin covered. I wasn't an idiot, so I listened to the walking, talking synthetic intelligence, and spoke with Zhalisee.

The healer was nice enough. She gave me the salve without many questions but was also busy. Cerridwen, who jumped into bed with her mate literally hours after arrival, was experiencing pregnancy symptoms. The healer and her apprentice were able to confirm that rather quickly. But they also didn't know what to expect from these pregnancies. So far, we'd learned these half-alien fetuses were intense, and the *V`òllø*'s gestation rate was faster. Luckily, no alien had claimed me, and I had the bottle of salve I needed in my hand.

I found my way to my favorite spot in Wupeso. With my legs dangling over the edge of the floating island and the smell of a salty sea breeze, I could feel my muscles relax. Unfortunately, relaxation only brought more attention to the fiery itch of my rash. Jerking the stopper from the bottle, the sharp menthol scent invades my nose. With two fingers, I gather enough salve to spread across the rash and hiss as the antiseptic ointment cleans the raw skin.

"That's still bothering you?" Aston asks, sitting close but not crowding. I stick the stopper back in the bottle and tuck it away, tugging the dress sleeve over my forearm.

"Well, it's not soothing me."

She rolls her eyes at me, keeping a reasonable distance from the edge. I find it ironic that 'Little-Miss-Bestie-to-The-Sky-Warriors' finds the edge petrifying. Like Rihu or Royi would let her fall. Certainly not her new extension of a best friend, Kano. In the last month, Aston had found a way to win everyone to her side of what we have dubbed 'The Mate Debate,' a political argument for written legislation allowing women to choose their mates in Wupeso. It would allow her to snub Llazho legally and force him to avoid her. I personally think Aston wanted more hoops for Llazho to jump through to prove his trainability. But, man-training aside, Aston was an extraordinary woman. She brought her skills from Earth to the land of Wupeso and turned Shojo on its head.

"I'm supposed to be the melodramatic one, Roxie."

"Well, you're doing a crap job," I reply, winking over my shoulder and resisting the urge to itch. I draw my gun and count the bullets to keep my hands busy. Twelve, three, and one.

Sixteen total. I ensure my weapon is ready to fire and tuck it back into the makeshift thigh holster I'd created.

"There's still sixteen bullets," Aston tells me, leaning back on her hands.

This had become a little bit of a tradition. Since neither one of us slept a whole night – me because of nightmares, her because of hate sex – we would meet up and watch the sunrise together. And chat. On Earth, I wasn't much of a chatter.

At home, my mother and older sister always held the conversation. They were pictures of femininity who knew how to hold a conversation, sit up straight, and look appealing. At work, you only spoke when spoken to. And I didn't have much social life outside of drinks with old war buddies. Those conversations never ran too deep. These ones on the island did, though. In the altered state of our floating island conversations, it was hard not to talk about the real stuff, and being on Shojo allowed the distance I needed to speak honestly. Which was something I never had on Earth, and would never give up.

"Do you miss your sister?" Aston asks, staring at the sky as it shifts from one unusual color to the next.

"Yes," My reply is honest but unsettling. "Satine and I were never close, but I miss her. She was still my sister."

"Me too. Well, not *your* sister, obviously. My brothers, though. Especially Parker. I remember this one time right before I applied for art school when…" Aston goes on to tell me a whole story about her and Parker and an awkward encounter with a male stripper that got them kicked out of some old-school Vegas establishment and banned for life. It's a funny story. She tells it, and I can hear the "Benny Hill Theme Song" as a soundtrack. Still, I don't laugh. No matter how often she paused to check, I listened and didn't laugh. No matter how many punchlines she throws, the best I can manage is a stiff tilt of my lips. After long enough, she gives up on getting me to laugh. Instead, she settled for asking me what I'd eat if we found ourselves back on Earth today.

"Spam Onigiri and kettle chips," I answer without hesitation. My answer surprised Aston, but she shook it off. She would eat some special avocado toast from a high-end bistro near her neighborhood.

Luckily, before I have to entertain more questions, the sun rises, silencing her as usual. Something about the sunrise on this planet makes me long for home. Maybe because it is so otherworldly. Instead of purples, blues, and reds, the sky fades from a deep red to a light lilac, striking a streak of sickly green through an otherwise stunning view. But the clouds are still white, and though this planet's sun is a touch lighter and larger than our earth's sun, it's comparable enough to overlook.

We sit silently for a while longer, enjoying the heat on our skin and the light on our faces. I soak in the moment. Right now, there are no evil monsters running amuck, no arguing soulmates, no nightmares. Instead, there is only a warm, tropical scent, a friend at my back, and a bright and shining new day. When the first official hour begins, I hear Aston stir behind me. If we don't move soon, we won't arrive at the loft in time to pretend we had been there the whole night. So, we both stand from our spots on the ground.

My head swirls, black dots swimming at the edges of my vision, but I push forward from the island's perimeter. Aston's copper brows pinch, but she doesn't offer to help me, knowing I'd refuse. I pause, leaning over my knees to drag in a breath, and the dots swirl away. I offer her a tight smile before straightening and sneaking back into the loft with her.

It's midday when I come to again. I wasn't feeling great when we got back to the loft, and with the sun up, sleep came easier.

Aston was kind enough to bring me some water and food. Both sit by my bedside, untouched. I force myself to eat the mushy cereal even though the smell of it makes my stomach churn. My mother would somehow know from lightyears away if I didn't feed my flu. Not that it would matter because my sickness would be my fault too. She would blame me since I wasn't sleeping and tell me the post-traumatic stress disorder was pretend. All in my head. She wouldn't tuck me into bed and let me rest. She would drag me out of bed to stick my face over a steaming rice bowl and demand I eat. So, I do.

It was not an easy feat, but I ate enough to keep my mother's voice from my mind. Then, I went out to join the rest of the women.

All of us were starting to adapt. With Kano and Vera married and the human faction settled, the *peholoe* were helping us integrate. We learned new skills, like foraging and cooking the foods of this planet, cultural cleanliness practices, weaving and sewing, and even the practical written *V`òllø* language.

Nelly and Cerridwen began teaching the children those skills first thing after breakfast and before the older kids went to warrior training. Once everyone was gone for the day, I would sneak off for my favorite lesson – flight.

The downside being I was near two of the flirtiest sky warriors on the planet. The upside was I got to enjoy the thrill of flying. That thrill would push away all the self-pity I had amassed since I realized I was stuck here. I fasten my thigh-holster to my leg and tighten it down before waving goodbye to the women in the loft. Aston shoots me what she believes to be a knowing wink before I disappear to meet with Royi again.

Rihu and Royi, who the women lovingly call the twins despite not being born brothers, are also incredible flirts. So, whenever I leave the loft to meet with them, Aston assumes it's for a different kind of riding lesson. Not the case. Rihu drives me too crazy to consider, and Royi is respectful during our studies.

He may throw a cheeky look at me when he gets me to crack a smile or place a well-timed compliment, but he's a professional during the actual training. Plus, I don't see them that way.

I mean, Royi is attractive. It would be a lie to say otherwise. His skin is a cool sage, with deep emerald tattoos curving over his biceps and chest. He keeps his hair, what one could call pistachio-blond, shorter on the sides and swoopy on the top. Like all the *V`òllø*, he's muscular and tall. But where Kethi and Kano are overwhelming, Royi is approachable – if you have to approach an alien.

When I arrive, he's bent over a workbench, fixing the ring on a harness. Tapping his shoulder, I set my face in a neutral position in preparation for his playful greeting. But when Royi sees my face, his smile drops.

"You look ill."

"And here I was thinking about how handsome you were," I spit, my lip curling. I cross my arms over my chest, and my hand itches to reach for my gun. It's been doing that a lot. If I had a therapist, I imagine they would say needing a weapon is a way to feel in control when I feel threatened. But I don't have a therapist, and I'm outnumbered. So, I don't put much weight behind that.

Royi's grin grows because even from an ill woman, a compliment will feed his ego. Ridiculous.

I snap, "Teach me something."

Royi flicks his tail in salute and turns to Lari. She is a beautiful creature. Like a crow or raven from Earth, she has long black feathers. They shimmer with a deep blue iridescence in the sunlight. Her beak is short and straight but capable of crushing through hard scales and shells. Unlike Earth crows, she is big and strong enough to ride into battle. Those alluring feathers cover an armored body and enough muscle to kill a *V`òllø*. Though, Lari never has.

Royi brags about how he raised her from when she was a hatchling. This turned out to be such an incredible feat because it took them an extra-long time to bond. Usually, the *V`òllø* would hunt the *uhichi* eggs and steal them from the mother. It's a form of mercy because the *uhichi* would otherwise try to eat their young. But Lari had already hatched and defended against its mother when Royi found her. He thought she would be a sweet, gentle mount, but when Royi picked her up, she attacked as her instincts determined. It took Royi three months to get her on his side. Soon after, they were history.

Now, Lari loves the *V`òllø*, and since the humans are friendly with the *V`òllø*, they are friendly with her.

Royi does a long, high whistle before dropping it with two clicks of his tongue. This is the command for Lari to come to attention, and she does. He does a low, short whistle, and she heels to his side. Next, with a triple click of his tongue, she prepares for harnessing. Because of the bird's size and build, it is easiest to harness her when she lies down. Padded loops of leather attach to smooth metal rings around the chest and over the wings. It included flexible stretches of woven material to allow freedom of movement without risking security. A wicker seat with bands of leather secures each leg to secure the primary rider. A secondary set of loops exists for an extra rider.

"We're not going up today if you're dizzy or nauseous," Royi says as I get the last few latches in place.

I itch the rash under my sleeve and shake my head, "I'm not dizzy or nauseous. Just tired."

He nods. Vera made it look easy the first time we flew. She took the hand offered and climbed into the saddle like she had been doing it her entire life. From watching her, I had been confident. Little did I know that even after a month of lessons, I would struggle to mount the beast alone. I was five foot one, half the size of some of the *V`òllø* men at the tops of their horns. My foot couldn't even reach the loop. Royi let me try, but when I couldn't manage, his hands came to my waist to lift me into place. Then, we were off.

In the air, Royi directs the bird with sounds. Up, whistle low, and then high. Down, whistle high and then low. Left, click, whistle. Right, whistle, click. As we fly, he explains how if Lari isn't given a command, she will fly intuitively in the safest pattern. Next, he indicates for me to try. I take my time, practicing each direction and feeling her surge and bank at my commands. When I feel like I have the hang of it, Royi directs me through the orders for landing her along the island's ledge.

I'm about to slide off when Royi says he has one more drill he wants me to run. Before I can strap back in, Royi tells me a whistle pattern and shoves me off Lari and over the ledge.

CHAPTER TWO
Kethi

"Go retrieve your *ĝha*," My mother demands, staring at the marks on my chest. Every so often, they burned, and I wondered if the human, Roxie, thought of me. It had been a complete cycle of the moons since I left the 'happy' Roxie back in Wupeso and returned to Valkarra. My people welcomed me home with bowed horns. I had returned to my usual duties as Rogeshu and Iritoena. Everything was back to normal. I slept in my bed, woke to my mother scratching at my door, worked throughout the day, and still, it did not feel like home.

My mother slides a bowl of my favorite foods before me. Warm roasted roots, tender game meat, and a slice of *ur'e gu*. I am lucky she is home during this time. She is not often in Valkarra, preferring to explore the surrounding area and travel to unexplored lands. My mother is a mapmaker first and a parent second. She left the child-rearing to my father and the city mostly. Only stopping in once in a moon cycle to ensure our happiness and remind us how she could cook better than our father. After my father died, she returned for a long time, only returning to exploration when the Baso Sheva demanded it. That demand is how she avoided the Death of Baso Sheva. I slide the food away.

"I am not hungry, mother. Thank you."

"Oh, please," She harrumphs, sliding it before me again. "You are merely heartsick. Rejection is not cause to starve."

I take a small bite of *ur'e gu* to please her, and I am frustrated when it pleases me too. I finish my plate, paying no mind to my mother's self-satisfaction. She dishes me a second slice of *ur'e gu* when Liro joins us. He is my younger brother and my advisor. He met Baso Sheva's blessing of humans with me, including Roxie. He has often said I am a fool for leaving her in

Wupeso for various reasons. He sees me sulking over my dish and grins.

"Thinking of Kano tending to your *ĝha*?" He chuckles even as my marks burn at the insinuation. This is his favorite reason to point out. It is untoward to allow another man to care for my *ĝha*, even if it is her preference. Still, I shove my brother's horn, growling in his direction.

"No rough-housing," Our mother snaps, sliding away our treats. Liro glares in my direction, sitting up tall and giving our mother a look of innocence. She is softer on him because he looks more like her. He has the darker blue skin and the icy markings. She tentatively slides his slice of *ur'e gu* before him. I look more like our father, who she misses dearly. Though my temperament, when I'm not suffering from the absence of my *ĝha*, is more like my hers. I stop glaring in Liro's direction and my mother gives me my second slice again.

"So sensitive, Valkarra's Rogeshu," Liro muses ignoring the warning look of our mother. He eats a bite of his food, chewing slowly. I chew slower. "I imagine your judgment is right, though. It is better for Miss Roxie to stay in Wupeso with a more powerful and faithful Rogeshu."

That's it. This time my mother doesn't intervene. I tackle Liro to the floor, my fangs gnashing for his face and neck. He catches my shoulders shoving me away. Tumbling across the floor, I roll to my feet, stalking across the room to stomp him until he is nothing but an imprint in the dirt, but he meets me on his feet with a feral grin. My fist swings as my vision blurs. A sheen of rage strengthens my resolve as Liro lands a fist against my bare side. My horns clash with his as we block and attack one another. I land an attack on his side and he shoves me away, but I keep coming. As I step in to punch him, his fist lands across my jaw and my *jisa* shudders.

Usually, I would feel it strengthen beneath a punch, but it doesn't. I'm so stunned; I don't see the second hit coming. Liro's fist slams into my face, destroying my *jisa* entirely and knocking me to the ground. I feel the bone of my nose crunch and the throbbing ache in my cheek.

"May Sheva strike you," I curse, spitting blood from the side of my mouth. Through my non-swelled eye, I can see Liro panting for breath. I try to force my *jisa* forward, but it refuses to cover my skin. I smack my arm, open my third eye, tap the marks on my chest but it won't come forth. Liro seems to notice it's absence and instead of capitalizing on his violence, concern knots his brows. My mother rushes to my side.

Panic envelops me as I stumble upward from the floor. Liro and my mother seem to know what to do, slinging my arms over their shoulders and exiting my home. The first sliver of the sun has yet to rise and there are only a few people heading toward the temple. Liro demands they wait outside as they drag me in. I half-walk, half-crawl toward the natural spires of crystal the temple is built around. Wrapping my arms around a twisted crystal of red and blue, I feel my *jisa* slowly grow and thicken back into place. But my face still throbs and my nose still bleeds. I look at Liro and my mother and they confirm with their looks. Something is wrong.

CHAPTER THREE
Roxie

"Ass," I rasp, my legs shaking as I stumble away from the ledge. I glare at Royi as he laughs, removing the harness from Lari. The mount responded quickly to my falling, or rather Royi's shoving, swooping low to gently pick me from the air. I was still hundreds of feet from the water when she had me in her grip. She would never have let me fall. After such an incredible catch, Lari showed her kind nature by ensuring my stability with a soft nudging of her beak.

"All sky warriors must experience it. I remember when my mother shoved me from her beast."

I wretch into the underbrush, steadying myself against a tree. I spit the taste of bile, wiping the edges of my mouth with my sleeve. A wave of dizziness strikes me, and the edges of my vision blacken again.

"I'm not a freaking sky warrior," I sputter, blinking rapidly to try and diminish the creeping urge to pass out.

"But you would like to be, yes? That's why you carry your small weapon and look over your shoulder as if you expect a beast behind you," Royi asks, carefully wrapping the harness straps to ensure they don't tangle.

I move a couple steps closer, sinking against a non-vomit tree and placing my head between my knees. I didn't want to be a sky warrior. I only liked to ride the *uhichi,* and I carried my gun everywhere. My hand flies to my thigh, and the moment of panic ebbs when I find it still securely in its holster. Popping it out, I check each magazine, relaxing entirely when I see the bullet in the chamber. I mentally count sixteen bullets.

The blackness around my vision fades as I ponder his question, but it's replaced with a deep ache in my head. I close my eyes, and the sound of bone crunching immediately fills my mind. It seems to echo around me, and the pain radiates from my nose across my cheekbone. What in the nine hells is going on with me? The pain leaves as fast as it came, but still, my head aches. I pull my hands to my temples, pressing in on my skull to find relief.

"Roxie?" Royi questions, leaning toward me. I can see he's in front of me, but his image doubles and wavers in front of my vision. I squeeze my eyes closed at the pain his voice causes.

"Roxie, are you okay?" He asks. His hands hit my shoulders, and the itching multiplies and burns. I can hear myself cry out as if I'm no longer in my body. I press my hands over my ears, tucking myself in to block out as much sound and light as I can. But it is still too loud and too bright. The pain is still forceful and sharp.

The disembodied feeling of his hands comes as he tucks me to his chest. Rihu's voice joins the cacophony of sound, splitting my head in half.

"Is she okay?"

"Get Zhalisee. Have her meet us at the loft."

The moment Royi's hands release me, a small wave of relief washes through me, only to be worsened by double when he presses a cool rag against my forehead.

My voice is raw when I whisper, "Stop. Stop."

Royi listens. Ripping the rag from my forehead, he turns back to his little tray of potions in search of a remedy. I hear Zhalisee and Rihu crowd into the room.

"What did you do?" She snaps, seeing the distress I'm in. I peek at her, but it makes my eyes ache, forcing them shut again. Her cool fingers rip up the sleeves of my tunic, and the rash is worse. Like the surface of water, lines of silver race across every inch of my rosy skin. Her voice grates my mind like the rest.

"I didn't do anything. We had our normal flying lesson, and everything was fine. I asked if she was dizzy or nauseous before her drop! I swear." Royi says, panic in his tone.

"Then, why do her eyes bleed red?"

A blissful moment of silence takes over. Then, Zhalisee shoves Royi out of the way, sending both him and Rihu off to collect her nurse. She looks at the tray of implements before looking back at me. Her smile is more of a grimace as her hands work to the bottom of my tunic. I do my best to uncurl and let her lift it from my body, baring my stomach and neck. Zhalisee's gasp has me peeking at my body, which is covered in the same silvery rash. Whatever I've contracted, it's not human because that is not normal.

The smell of menthol permeates the room, sinking into my nostrils and adding an extra sensory nightmare for my aching head to process. It does a lousy job, returning the input with pain throughout my body. Zhalisee's helper shows up with Daria behind him. I watch his eyes widen, and Daria's head tilt with curiosity. And suddenly, Zhalisee shouts for them to help her. They work together, and I feel their foreign hands rubbing the salve into my skin, whispering over what this could possibly be.

"She's boiling," Daria blurts, yanking her hand from my forehead and pressing two fingers to my pulse. "And her heart rate is working double-time."

I groan at the contact, and her hand snaps away from me. Disbelief enters her voice when she says, "She shocked me."

Zhalisee's confusion is evident in her voice as she looks through her bag of tinctures and potions. Every time she lands on something, her apprentice rattles off a reason why it won't work. The salve soothes the itch, not the pain, and I force my eyes open. They flash between the three medics in the room as Zhalisee reveals a bottle of Helleboralis spores. I shake my head. I know what those do. Those made Vera so horny she ended up in an alien's bed for the night.

"It could work," Her apprentice says, "The Helleboralis heats the blood. It could kill whatever virus ravages her and give her the pleasure she needs to stave off the pain."

"You can't dose her with alien ecstasy," Daria defends. "She needs actual medical care. Where's Blossom?"

I nod at Daria's words, but moving my head and neck sends another sharp pain down my spine. My teeth crunch together. Daria leaves the room, and the clacking of the crystal beads sends a hum of musical *tings* through the space. They clash along my skin like hail pelting me, and I curl in on myself again.

"We can't wait for Blossom," the apprentice says, nervously glancing between the bottle of spore juice and Zhalisee. She nods in agreement. I shake my head at them, but Zhalisee doesn't care. Wrestling my hand from my face, she tugs my chin down and tilts the tincture into my mouth.

It works like a charm. The happy drugs release rapidly into my system, heating my blood and relaxing my muscles. My skin still burns slightly, but the pain in my head fades to a dull throb, and I can open my eyes. I feel them drooping, and my muscles become jelly, extra tired from how tight I held them clenched. My groans turn to moans, and embarrassment curves through me.

On Earth, I never dabbled in recreational drugs. I abstained from everything, even weed, and alcohol. Satine had been the wild child, and because she was the favorite, she got away with stashing a fifth of vodka in her closet. The one time I had a sip of beer with my dad's permission at a family function, my mother had a conniption. She went into a whole lecture about how I would become a drunkard and not amount to anything. For God's sake, the woman didn't even allow me sugar.

And now, I understood why. This was bliss. I felt like I was floating. All the pain previously frying my nerves turned to pleasure, and it felt like I was a popsicle melting in the hot sun. I was a fresh pool of tiger's blood snow cone, ready to be sipped from a tiny pointed cup. The feather mattress beneath me felt like a pool floaty, and everything felt right.

My body uncurled, spreading out atop the fresh linen sheet beneath me. Zhalisee and her apprentice melted away. I heard the mechanical extension of Blossom's legs and the tap of her metal feet against the floor. Finally, the beads shook, and Daria and Blossom were there. Daria's face twisted in anger.

"You gave her the Helleboralis?"

"Helleboralis has an unexpected and potentially dangerous effect on humans," Blossom spouts, regurgitating fact upon fact about the substance's reaction in our fragile human bodies. Mm, body. My eyes close, and a specific body comes to mind.

The body is covered in an expanse of skin the color of Earth's summer sky. Silver lines spiral across his veined forearms, drawing my attention to his long masculine fingers. Those are fingers I would love to have all over me.

Cold, skinny hands tap my face, and I see Blossom's lavender eyes staring down at me. The chill of her metal skin hurts, but the pleasure drug keeps the worst of it away. My body's heat seems to bend, but it doesn't leave. It wanes, focusing its energy on keeping the pain away instead of creating fantasies of men who aren't even here.

Blossom's eyes scan my body with her fancy medical tech, and she recites a bunch of medical mumbo jumbo before dumbing it down for the rest of us.

"Since this illness is not an Earth illness, I deduced this; The rash keeps her pain sensors firing, which overwhelms her mind and body. She should be feeling dizzy, nauseous, sharp pain. I cannot deduce the origin of the rash. I would like to draw blood."

My body chills, and the pain returns. I don't know if the Helleboralis is gone or if the idea of Blossom sticking a needle in my air-tender skin is the problem. Regardless, with the threat of the pain, I nod my head, offering my arm for a vein. There's a tiny pinch, and she's done, leaving Zhalisee to stamp the puncture wound with a tuft of clean cloth. Their hands on my skin make it ache, but the pain is still dull.

"After testing the Helleboralis, I injected you with a small dose of pain medication. There is a low chance of side effects from the combined drugs, including fever, swelling, chills, and vomiting. If you start convulsing, send someone for me," Blossom doesn't pause to confirm I've understood in my drug haze before jumping into her breakdown of my disease. "The rash is of alien origin, containing many of the same compounds as the *V`òllø* blood and *jisa*. It seems you have a soulmate. Congratulations."

"Vera didn't have any of these symptoms from her," Daria pauses, "Situation."

"Vera did not resist her bond."

"I'm not resisting a bond," I snap, forcing myself to sit up in bed. My body is weak, but I refuse to let that deter me. With a grunt, I find myself propped against the wall behind me.

I admitted to myself on occasion that I liked how Kano loved Vera. I liked how he protected her and looked at her as if she were his goddess reincarnate. It wasn't like I was actively looking for a *ĝha*, but if I found a person to treat me the way Kano treats Vera, I would be all for it.

"You must be," Blossom spouts.

"What about Aston? She's been resisting her bond with Llazho. Shouldn't she be sick too if this is the case?"

A shiver works down my spine. I know Aston is publicly resistant, but she sneaks out to be with Llazho every night. Even if she hates him, she spends time with him. Aston fights with him every night but ends up sleeping in his bed. She always sneaks back out to meet me for the sunrise and swears she hates him, detailing all the little quirks about him that piss her off. She spends the day forcing him further away and caves when the moon comes out. Zhalisee, Daria, and Blossom try to figure it out, and I stay silent. I won't break Aston's confidence over a medical theory.

"I promise I don't have a soulmate," I say instead, my voice still raw from the earlier pain, "I would know."

I would know, wouldn't I? There would be signs for me to follow. I would want to be near him, jump his bones, talk, and spend time with him. Right? I visualize the men of the island, and not one of them brings a tug to my heart. As I'm about to give up, the image comes unbidden to my mind.

"If perchance you weren't happy here, or you thought you might be happier elsewhere, I'd love to bring you to Valkarra."

I'd been so defensive when he asked I spluttered out a no so venomous it read more like, "Get fucked." Worse, I looked at his face, all fallen, and doubled down.

"I wouldn't want to go anywhere with you. How dare you try to isolate me, drag me away from the other humans. No. I will never go to Valkarra."

Kethi gave me a small, broken smile and stood from the ground. Brushing the crumbs of his cake from his trousers, he nodded in deference before leaving me standing on the ledge, staring after his slumped shoulders.

I decided here and now, Kethi would have told me if he was my soulmate.

"Your blood says you do," Blossom replies sharply. "If you would like, I can show you the comparisons to Vera and Cerridwen's tests."

Blossom projects the charts onto the wall and Daria's head tilts as she looks at the chemical levels in their blood versus mine. I can see when she determines the blood must be right because she nods, facing me.

"Girl, you're mated, *ĝha*'ed up. Soulmate found."

I look to Zhalisee and their apprentice. They nod, glancing between the human charts and the evidence written into my skin.

"The rash does look like *jisa's* protective pattern," Zhalisee says.

"And the headache is in line with a *ĝha* reaching out but unable to connect to the other."

"I'm not mated," I splutter, my eyes widening. "There's no tattoo," I say, tugging my shirt collar down. Daria gasps, hands coming to her mouth, and Zhalisee's mouth twitches into a smile.

I look down at my body, and sure enough,   a bright black and silver tattoo sits right where it should.

CHAPTER FOUR
Kethi

I didn't leave the temple until my brother returned from Wupeso. To keep myself strong and protected, I stayed in the strengthening presence of the Baso Sheva and prayed. If my growing faith surprised my people, they did not show it. Simply leaving me to do my prayer as they shuffled in and out of the temple over the days. My mother brought me meals, though I could tell she was itching to leave town once again and return to her studies. It was the third day, the final meal when Liro arrived.

Stealing a bite from my plate, he collapsed into a wooden pew, tilting his head back with a sigh. His features, pulled taut, relaxed with each moment he spent within our holy space. He flinched when I spoke.

"What of Roxie?"

"Your *ĝha* is quite ill. They have been parading the men before her trying to locate her *ĝha* to help her feel better."

Rage like I had never known burned in my chest, spurring me forward. I left the temple, shouting orders. I called for Nohktir, ordered Liro to bring me my mount. Sent my mother to collect traveling rations and clean clothes for me. I washed my face in the cool stream, preparing to go straight to my *ĝha*. I was fine to leave her in Wupeso when I knew she did not want to leave the other women. I could understand her distaste with my original proposal. But I would not leave her to fall sick and die from our distance. She is my *ĝha* and I would not let her wither away.

"What are you going to do when we reach Wupeso?" Nohktir asks, harnessing his beast beside me.

"I will do what I am best at. Negotiate."

The sun is rising when we arrive in Wupeso. Only a half-day's hard ride away from my island, the distance should not have made Roxie so sick in such a small time. It should not have made her sick at all. Soul sickness was myth. A fear tactic used by the *peholoe* to ensure *ĝhajo* remained together as the Baso Sheva intended. Or at least I believed that until I flew past the floating island holding my *ĝha* and heard her groan of pain. My *jisa* flickered before staying in place and I let out a breath of relief. I am here now. I would fix this.

Rihu and Royi Tisugo meet me at the island's edge, hands on their weapons.

"This is unexpected," Rihu says, grinning like a fool as I try to keep my glaring minimal. "Twice in one season. I would have worn my nicer bloomers if I knew you were coming."

His counterpart, Royi, rolls his eyes, but doesn't speak against him.

"I need to speak with – "

"Kano. Yes, we know," Rihu says, his grin dropping.

"Post-haste, I would imagine," Royi smirks, turning away from the ledge to lead me through the village. They lead me across the bridge and past the *peholoe* loft where the human women sleep. It would be so simple for me to pop in and check on Roxie and I want to. But the Tisugo drag me along right past the trail without letting me get a word in.

When I glance back at the loft, Rihu simply says, "The women are sleeping. They need their rest."

"How are they?" I ask, even though Roxie is the only one I wish to ask after.

"Many of the women are well," Royi responds, his smirk growing. My mark burns beneath my shirt as we get further from my *ĝha* and my muscles stiffen, trying to draw me back toward her. The men tell me about many of the women. Daria, the nurse, and how wonderful she's been to Zhalisee, their healer. They tell me about Aston and Llazho, the *V`òllø* are shocked by the human's ire but their respect for women won't let them speak against it. Then, they provide the most shocking update.

One of the human women is expecting a *V`òllø* child. The healers and their metallic friend both agree the child will be viable. I stop in my tracks, but we are already moments from Kano's door. A beast is sleeping beside his home, snuffling into his garden bed and my hand holds my weapon, but Rihu and Royi ignore it as they approach.

Kano meets them at the door. In hushed tones, they tell him about my arrival and he carefully pads across his land toward me. In a low tone, he says, "My Vera and Magnus are sleeping. You would not like to wake either. Let's take this to the crystal fields."

When we finally settle there, Kano says a quick prayer before turning to me, "What can I help you with this fine morning?"

I want to tell him to force Roxie to accompany me back to Valkarra, show him my *ĝha* mark, and steal her away, but her words come spinning back to me.

"No," She pauses, "No. I wouldn't want to go anywhere with you. How dare you try to isolate me, drag me away from the other humans. No. I will never go to Valkarra."

It had felt like a million tiny cuts opened across my skin, bleeding me out in front of her. Somehow, after years of practice, I maintained my composure and left her on the floating island as she wished. Somehow, I woke the next morning and departed for my home and I went an entire moon cycle without seeing her.

"I would like the women to visit Valkarra."

This isn't the exact truth. I would like Roxie to stay in Valkarra, but I must start somewhere I believe Kano will meet me. The easiest option is a visit. If I were to try and negotiate splitting the human population, I would have pushback from the humans and Kano. If I were to suggest only taking Roxie, I am not certain she would ever forgive me and my men would be disappointed in the outcome.

"I would like another magical space-pod filled with women to land for my men. Or for My Vera to have chosen a more docile pet. My point is, we all want things, Kethi. But only the Baso Sheva's will be done."

"I will allow our few available women to visit Wupeso in exchange."

"You do not have the number of women we do," He states plainly, throwing my words from a mere season ago back in my face. Suddenly, I remember why I hate negotiations, especially from a place of weakness.

"Yes, but I have five your village does not who could come to visit while your women are in Valkarra."

"While only five of Wupeso's women are in Valkarra."

"Five available women," I clarify, not wanting to waste time bringing Llazho's *ĝha* or the woman Pa has set his sights on to Valkarra. Of course, they could visit of their own accord, but we were obviously negotiating for the benefit of our villages.

"That would exclude my *ĝha*, Aston, Alba, Cerridwen, and Roxie," He tells me. His tone is informative, but the primal parts of my mind don't hear it. They only hear Kano intended to keep my *ĝha* from me.

"No, Roxie is mine," I growl, realizing my mistake. Kano grins in my direction, turning back to his prayers as I gather myself. I've never been emotional in this manner. I've always been able to set aside my emotions for negotiations and come out on the winning side.

"Why don't you take Roxie and leave the rest of the women in Wupeso with their friends and family?" Kano's tone is curious, and I struggle to avoid my annoyance. I do not want to be Kano's friend. We are both leaders and both of us have the right to do what is best for our people. This puts us at odds as often as it makes us allies. And his obvious misunderstanding of both his human population and my city's expectations grates my *jisa*.

"Roxie does not want to leave Wupeso," I grit out.

"Then, she does not have to," Kano replies.

"I can't leave her again."

"Don't leave, then."

"Kano – "

"Oh, Jesus! My bad."

Our heads snap toward the human woman standing at the entrance to the place of worship. She has brown hair tucked into a bun at the back of her head and wears a boring linen dress. She presses her hand against her chest and I can hear her heart beating from here. She holds no interest to either of us. So, Kano waves off her apologies and motions to the free prayer mats in the space. She is awkward and quiet as she finds a place to sit, arranging her skirts around her in the chosen spot. She glances between us and the crystals and the sky, her lips twitching between a smile and confusion.

"Uhm, am I interrupting something? I can come back later."

"Priscille, right?" Kano asks, smirking in my direction.

"Ah, yeah." Her brows furrow.

"You are human. You can help us. Kethi Rogeshu wants some of the women to visit his village, Valkarra. What do you think?"

She looks to the sky again and I pray in my heart that the Baso Sheva is on my side this moment. I pray this woman tells Kano she would like to visit and the human women would love to go. I pray the human women share the *V`òllø*'s sense of adventure.

"With Roxie so sick, and Cerridwen pregnant, I don't know how realistic the travel is. But I know I would love to. Valkarra has a real temple, don't they? I heard one of the men speaking of it during your *r¨uṣad'ù.*"

Her obvious excitement at the prospect of our temple is the part I fixate on. If I can convince one human, the rest will come.

"Yes, we built a temple to our Baso Sheva. It is built of the finest materials around the largest crystal spires in our lands."

Her eyes widen. She looks at Kano and her face returns to a usual level of expression. She crosses her arms over her chest and turns her attention to the crystals before her.

"Well, I am interested, but not alone. You could always ask the women what they want to do. I'm sure the human council will tell you," She shrugs.

Kano smiles, "A wonderful idea, Priscille."

I am left wondering, wonderful for who?

CHAPTER FIVE
Roxie

I feel much better. And I find that suspicious. Slowly, I open my eyes to peek at the room around me. The medical apprentice is asleep in a chair in the corner of the room, but no one else is around. For a moment, I wonder if he's my mate since every male in the entirety of Wupeso has been marched before me, and none have stopped the pain. But it doesn't hurt now.

I look down at the new ink on my chest and grimace. How does that work? I end up on an alien planet, and it can choose to give me a new tattoo? Moving lower, I moved the waist of my pants and checked to make sure my actual tattoo was still there. It was.

The tiny sun with sunglasses made me smile, and I climbed out of bed on a good note. Grabbing clean clothes from the box beneath the bed, I slip out of the bedroom and into the bathhouse.

The water is warm, and it soothes my muscles. It seemed to wash away all the sweat and dirt I'd acquired over my illness. It washes away the out-of-control feelings and the remaining buzz from the pain medicine. I wash my hair with minty-smelling soap and feel the minerals of the pool sink into my skin. A bath might not seem important right now since I'm on a happy commercial break from pain, but it was absolutely what I needed.

When I'm dried and dressed, I find myself sitting at the breakfast table, ravenous. The first few days on Shojo were misleading because Kano was determined to win the hearts of the humans. So, they would bring massive breakfasts all the way up to the *peholoe* loft for the women. Everything would already be prepared and laid out with fresh flowers and a bowl of crystal-clear water. We would all sit and eat and talk together. Since Kano and Vera got married, food delivery has slowed down. Instead of all sitting together and feasting on the food provided, the *peholoe* taught us how to trade in the market, and we all pitched in to bring food back to the loft. This ended in much smaller breakfasts and everyone eating at different times of the morning.

Since only Hoga and I were awake, I made us both a bowl of a creamy, yogurt-like substance and some of those cake-batter fruits. She sprinkled the *okkoran* dust on top of hers and didn't say a word of thanks. That's normal for her. We eat silently, and when I'm done with my first bowl, I return for seconds. And finally, thirds. Some of the other girls are waking up and getting food together for themselves and their siblings as I'm finishing my third bowl.

Everyone, especially Aston, is surprised and delighted to see me up and moving.

"She has risen!" Aston shouts, making the baby squawk in her direction. She tugs me into an unwelcome hug, and I tap her side lightly so she will release me. She beams as she dives into another ranting story, "So, you're never going to believe who I saw flying into town this morning."

"Kethi Rogeshu," Priscille answers, a pretty but plain woman who does not speak much.

"How'd you know?" Aston asks, using her hands and expression to say, 'Can you believe this woman? Priscille, keeping the gossip from us.'

"They were in the crystal fields this morning speaking about having some human women visit Valkarra."

I imagine Kethi knelt on one of the mats, impatiently waiting to speak with Kano about his hope for a visit. He was probably pushy and diplomatic. Trying to make it seem like Kano's idea, the same way he made it seem like it was my idea.

"If perchance you weren't happy here, or you thought you might be happier elsewhere, I'd love to bring you to Valkarra."

"Sonofabitch," I murmur as it all comes together. "He's the guy! Kethi is my freaking soulmate."

Everyone looks at me, confused, except Aston. She's grinning from ear to ear. He invited me to Valkarra because he wanted to be near me. I was sick because he left me here. I feel better because he's in town. Why is he in town? He's back probably because he was ill, too, or maybe because he heard about me being sick. And now he wants multiple women to come to Valkarra to get me there. But it won't work because I didn't ask for a *ĝha*. Especially not one who didn't tell me we were even together. And I don't want to go to Valkarra. Aston must see my face because her political march begins.

"Welcome to the mate-hate club."

"Mate-hate?" Priscille murmurs, confusion in her tone.

"Oh, yeah," Aston begins, getting warmed up for a big speech. "Mate-Hate Club, for those of us human women who didn't ask for an alien mate and sure as shit aren't any better for it."

"Language," Alba reprimands, arching a brow from the doorway. Pa is right behind her, rocking the baby in his arms and smiling at its squishy face. Aston waves her off, grin growing. She turns to the single women gathered together this morning with her arms outstretched.

"Have you or someone you know been victimized by this sacred soulmate bond? Yes, which is why you should join the mate-hate club. Because we come from a planet and culture where we choose our mates, not some unknown entity in the sky. And our culture is as important as the culture of the *V`òllø* people if we are going to work together in this community. As part of the mate-hate club, you will stand on the human side of the argument where legislation detailing what a *V`òllø* man can and can't do with an unaccepting human partner is laid out and negotiated for."

"I was already on the human side," Daria says, pointing to the purple nail color Aston had declared her campaign color.

"Me too," Priscille adds. "I'm always on the human side."

"Ladies, there shouldn't be sides. We are stuck here, and the *V`òllø* are our allies," Alba rebuts.

"Yes, our allies," Aston agrees, "But allies try to keep the peace. It is in our best interest to have rights against this soulmate bond to keep the peace."

"You're not going to like this," Priscille murmurs. She shoves a bite of food into her mouth and points at the door.

CHAPTER SIX
Roxie

Nope. This better not be happening. Kano, Kethi, and Liro all stand at the entrance to the *peholoe* loft like a brigade of men who have already decided for the women they rule. Kano's eyes scan the women, and a gentle smile overtakes his face to see we are all here. I watch in horror as Vera comes up the walkway with Magnus by her side. She leaves him at the entry to stand beside Kano. She smiles up at him, utterly oblivious to the impending conversation. Her pet, Magnus, lets out a whiny growl, choosing to lie down in the entry behind them.

Kethi's eyes burn into me, and I refuse to look at him. If he thinks I'm going to Valkarra because he dragged Kano into this, he's wrong. I'm not going anywhere without the other humans. He locked his eyes on me, and I could feel his discomfort as I looked anywhere but him. Rihu and Royi join the men, and my eyes find Royi. With my eyes, I try to beg him to get me out of this. My 'help-me' eyes only garner confusion from him until he realizes I'm glancing between him and Kethi, and he takes it as an opportunity to whisper something in Kethi's ear.

Kethi's eyes widen, and he bares his fangs in a snarl when Kano calls attention to the room.

"Humans, *peholoe*, I'm glad you are all here. Kethi Rogeshu of Valkarra has proposed a visitation to his village across the seas. The woman, Priscille, encouraged me to ask if you would like to visit. What do you think?"

The room is silent for a moment as the women look at one another. The question weighs on the room, and the *peholoe* knowingly stay out of it. I know silent conversations are passing around me, but I'm too concerned with the one I'm holding with Aston. She caught my eye when the question was out, and we'd been going back and forth since.

You should go, Aston's eyes say, alight at the prospect. *I'll go with you.*

I'm not going, I respond with a shake of my head to punctuate the point. My eyes flick to Kethi and roll.

Her eyes narrow in my direction, a smile tilting her lips. She raises her brows and tilts her head in his direction before starting a slow nod. Oh, no. I glance at the other women in the room, still silently deliberating.

Aston opens her mouth, "I – "

"I'll go," I interrupt, immediately regretting it. Cursing under my breath, I look to Kethi – who is beaming – and bring my fisted hands toward my face. Using my hands to block my face from his flabbergasted stare, I look at Aston, who choked on her stifled laughs. All alone on this mission, I roll my shoulders back and repeat myself. "I'll go to Valkarra."

Kethi stares at me, snapping his jaw closed and nodding. I can feel his eagerness though he doesn't show it. He was trained better. While the women feel the pressure of my statement, he waits silently. Following Kano's lead and practicing his diplomacy, he sets his eyes forward, locked on mine.

"Me too. I'll go too," Priscille offers, stepping forward from her place at the table. She smooths down her skirt, probably imagining the supposed temple already. Kethi keeps his eyes on me.

"I'm in," Clara adds, facing the general crowd. Kethi's eyes still don't stray.

"I want to go too," Aston chimes in, her smile so bright its light couldn't be contained. Kethi nods almost imperceptibly, but his eyes never leave my face.

The other women are silent. Daria's younger sister, Demi, speaks in hushed tones to her sister, gesticulating wildly with her arms. Zach holds both the twins' wrists as they try to tug away. The babe is asleep in the crook of Pa's elbow, and he locks his other arm around Alba's waist.

Three women. I have a team of three women; one is already mated. Kethi is still *staring* at me.

"When do we leave?" Aston asks, bouncing on the balls of her feet. I could never understand where she got her energy.

"You will leave tomorrow at sunrise," Kano announces. "And three *V`òllø* women will come to visit in your absence."

"It's like a student exchange program," Priscille says, her tone light. "I did one of those in high school. It was fun then too."

Kano nods to the room, and people start to dissipate. Kethi's eyes are locked on me, and I start backing away slowly. I keep him in my peripheral as I search for an exit strategy. *Why didn't I do this the first night I slept here?* I start to step down the hallway. *Maybe I'll take the back door of the bathhouse down to the floating island. Perhaps a flight will clear my head.*

I wasn't ready to talk to him. He didn't get to come here, pull this stunt, and then act like we were all hunky-dory. He could wait until I was ready - or better yet, until tomorrow.

Aston sidles up beside me, "Llazho's going to be pissed." Her words and tone didn't match. It would have felt more natural if she said she had won the lottery. Between her Mate-Hate Club and the sheer amount of fight she put up, you wouldn't expect her to have much zeal. I would find it exhausting. Glancing over my shoulder, I catch Kethi politely skirting his way through the women to follow me. I find this exhausting.

"Yes, you've done an amazing job pissing him off thus far. You have topped your evil genius," I reply, keeping one eye on the Valkarran and the other on my friend.

She continued telling me how she had only gotten started on the nine circles of hell she planned to put Llazho through. And I would nod at each evil point and offer my strategic expertise. My ideas would spur her on, and she would rattle off new ideas with exhilaration growing in her eyes. The whole time, I think about how to escape my mate, who is closing in on us. Aston is not dense, she knows exactly what I'm doing, and that's why she's so close. She's acting as a secondary barrier, as I do with her and Llazho whenever we have to attend something in public. While I'm grateful for it, she's also impeding my speed.

"I'm going for a quick flight. Since I won't get one for a while," I mutter, interrupting another great plan the redhead laid out. She nods in understanding, making sure to 'accidentally' run into Kethi as I slip into the bathhouse.

I hear Aston's cheery words, "Kethi Rogeshu! Gosh, long time no talk..."

Her words die as the door closes behind me. I rush across the stone-tiled floors, cursing the loud slap of my feet as it echoes through the chamber. Still, I walk with purpose, glancing back over my shoulder. My hand closes around the outer door as I hear the inner door click open. Kethi scans the space, and our eyes lock for only a second. A devilish smile turns his lips. I curse myself for the small squeak that leaves my body and force myself outside.

They built the *peholoe* loft far above the ground. The entry winds upward into the trees at a surprisingly manageable incline for how high up I find myself. The tiny balcony has no railing, and I halt mere inches from the ledge. Staring down, I catch sight of a safety net below while walkways in the trees break out from left to right. *Always choose the right, Honey.* My mother's voice whispers in my ear, and I twist toward the boards leading through the righthand trees.

I'm barely thirty feet away when I hear the door open again, and Kethi joins me outside.

"Roxie," His voice is like a cool glass of water on a hot day. The way he says my name is full of relief. Peace wends its way through my blood, and I armor my heart against it. He knew he was my mate and didn't tell me. He took away my choice. I got sick because of him. I hasten my steps. A curved ladder appears at the end of the walkway, and I keep my eyes locked on it.

"Roxie, please. Speak with me," Kethi begs. I can feel him behind me, mere inches from being able to grab me, and I pick up my pace, half-sprinting down the steps.

"No time. Flying lessons with Royi," I spout, acting as if my heart is not beating out of my chest. The logical part of me wants to escape. I know I can't fight him, and my instincts won't let me use my gun. None of this makes any sense. He shouldn't have this power over me. He doesn't own me. But the illogical part of me wants him to catch me. It wants him to pin me to a tree and kiss me, nip my bottom lip with his fang, hold me against his hard body. Arousal shoots through me. I try to blink away the image, feeling my feet hit the forest floor. From there, I run.

I don't mean I jog like I'm warming up with my military buddies. I mean, I run. It's like I'm the final girl in a slasher flick, running like I'm about to set the record Olympic pace. I fly through the trees, angling toward the floating island, ducking behind trees in hopes of losing him. I run like a twelfth-century maiden in a flowing white dress in the rain, trying to escape the sexualization of my body. Trying to outrace my thoughts, I don't hear when he catches up.

His body slams against mine, and we sprawl to the forest floor. We fall so hard that my hair goes flying in all directions. His arms band tightly around me, and he tucks his body around me, taking the brunt of our fall. His hot exhalation blows over my face as I try to wiggle my way out of his arms. I'm sliding down his body, and I feel his hardness growing beneath me. Wicked images flick through my mind, and I double down on my efforts.

"Good girl, Roxie. Fight me," He growls. He moves faster than I expected, loosening his grip on me. I rip backward out of his arms and tumble to the undergrowth. He uses my momentum against me, crawling over my body and trapping me beneath him. I am panting for breath, scrambling from the cage of his body. Frustration and arousal mix as my heart beats erratically. But I won't give up. I reach my arm between his, planning to twist away, but his hand catches my wrist.

Snatching my other wrist, he pins them in one of his massive hands above my head. My chest arcs towards him, and I curse my nipples as they pebble beneath my tunic. His eyes rake down my body, the blue color flaring when they land on the juncture of my thighs. I am embarrassingly wet, and somehow, he can tell. My cheeks heat at his perusal. When his eyes meet mine, I gasp.

Prince Charming is gone. The hopeful, seeking eyes from earlier are replaced with a focused, predatory gaze. Kethi's arms are tense above me. The veins jump as he presses my wrists further into the ground. He spreads my legs, pressing his thigh against my core. My hips roll, and I bite my lip to stifle my moan. He peels his upper lip back, revealing his fangs, and my nerves double.

"Kethi," I say breathlessly. He groans. My pussy pulses at the deep reverberation.

"Kethi, please," I beg. "Think about what you're doing."

His lips press gently to my throat, and his tender touch softens my body. I feel the gentle drag of his fang on the sensitive spot behind my ear before his lips press against it. My hips buck in response. His hot voice is in my ear, sending goosebumps over my spine.

"And what am I doing, Roxie?" He nips my earlobe, prying a moan, unbidden, from me. He's a monster, barely contained. He doesn't cross any lines as he teases circles along my hipbone, gently kissing and nipping his way down my neck and chest. His lust-addled eyes track mine with every move he makes, cataloging my reactions.

I'm past all thought, grinding against his thigh, when I beg, "Kethi, please."

"Please, what? Use your words," His free hand skirts up my side, leaving a trail of pleasure in its wake. I throb when he growls, "Tell me what you want, Roxie."

Frantic for some kind of stimulus, some type of pressure, I grind against his thigh, sputtering, "T-touch me."

The leash snaps, and Kethi sucks my pointed nipple through my tunic, using his free hand to tease the other. All the remaining aches from my illness vanish under his ministrations. He releases my hands with a deep command, "Leave them above your head."

He tugs my pants from my body, tossing them to the wayside, before sliding his hands under my tunic. The fabric crinkles above his hands, baring my body to him in its entirety. He leans back to admire, and I go to move my hands. His growl halts me in place. I search his face. His eyes are so overtaken in the light blue glow I can't find his pupil, and his chest rises and falls with rapid breath. Those stunning eyes leave a trail of goosebumps in their wake, and I struggle to remain still as he clocks the tiny sun tattoo on my hip.

"You're beautiful, Roxie."

His words are so genuine it throws me off guard. And Kethi doesn't give me a chance to recover. His hand wraps around an ankle, spreading it wide. He kisses right above the bone and along my calf. My goosebumps spread, prickling out from the heat of his breath along my skin. He works his way up my leg, and it feels good. My nerves fire with pleasure, a complete antithesis to the pain of the last couple of days. Finally, he reaches the apex of my thighs. His hot breath coasts across my skin, and I moan in anticipation.

I don't recognize my voice when I moan, "More."

"Like this?" He answers, his voice husky before he licks my pussy from entrance to clit.

"Yes!" I exclaim, my hips writhing off the forest floor. I can hear the sharp snap of twigs beneath me, but poking and prodding fade as Kethi lies between my legs. He teases my clit with his tongue, observing my reactions. Sliding one of his long, thick fingers into me, I jerk. I pin my hand to my mouth to stifle my moan, and Kethi stops his ministrations. His hand is paused inside me, his face inches from my dripping cunt.

Shaking his head gently, he says, "Hands above your head, Sunshine."

It takes effort to drag my hand back to its place above me, pushing out my chest. Kethi's hot breath brushes against my sensitive mound as he waits patiently to resume. Part of me says I've lost myself. I should stop this now. But that part is overridden by my curiosity about what it will be like to come on Kethi's hot tongue. I cross my wrists above my head, stretching them out long. Then, when my hands are high above me, and I'm wiggling impatiently, he curls his fingers inside and sucks on my clit.

I've built a small, quiet chant of "Yes, yes, yes." This is so right; it's so good. I can feel my body relaxing as the bond works its magic – the effects of the intimacy with Kethi doubling down on my pleasure. Kethi works my sensitive pussy, driving it higher and higher toward my release. I'm panting and writhing, and he holds an arm across my hips, growling against me, sending pleasureful vibrations across my skin. His eyes are blown wide, staring at mine. I can hear his words in my mind.

Come for me, Roxie. Come all over my face.

His fingers rub my G-spot, his tongue flicks my clit, and the pressure builds. I crest the ridge of my completion and crash over it. My scream of pleasure rattles the trees, and I feel him groan against me, licking my wetness with fervor. His fingers don't stop as he escorts me through my orgasm, tasting and devouring me.

When he's done, it feels like the island shifts. He sits back on his knees before me as my chest rises and falls erratically. I try to catch my breath, and he watches carefully. We're both silent. Tentatively, I trail my arms down and across my chest, sitting up and plucking a leaf from my hair. His cheeks become silver, and he spins around to grab my tunic. He helps me into it, stretching it over my head. I shove my arms through the sleeves, and Kethi draws my hair from the neck of my tunic. It's longer than I usually keep it.

I always kept my hair at exactly shoulder length. The perfect length to keep it off my neck and tie it up for work. When I put it down, it would frame my face right, and it never became unmanageable when I kept it above my shoulders. Now, it was inches past them. I needed to cut it before the *SS Herculean,* but my mom had something urgent she needed my help with, and we didn't get to cut it.

My mom. Guilt slams into me. What would she think of what I just did? I snatch my pants from the bark of a tree, sliding them over my legs. Kethi is still dressed and kneeling, staring at me as if he's dealing with guilt of his own.

His voice is gruff and broken when he says, "I'm sorry, Roxie."

Rage instantly heats my blood. I want to scream at the man. What is he sorry for? Is he sorry for leaving me here when he knew we were mates? Is he sorry for what we did in the woods? Or is he sorry he's my mate? Instead of yelling, I pluck another twig from my hair and keep my questions to myself.

In the coolest, most composed voice I can muster, I say, "It's fine. It's not like it meant anything."

His jaw tightens. My rash itches. The hardness pressing against his pants fades. He looks up at me from beneath his silver lashes, and my breath halts in my chest. I had never seen a *V`òllø* man hurt, but I imagined it would look like that if I had. Kethi seemed like I'd torn his heart out and handed it back to him.

He considers his words before a smirk tilts his lips. He stands from the ground and crowds me against the tree at my back. He's staring down at me, and his eyes waver from wide to pointed, focusing at different points on my face. Fear makes my heart pound, and I wonder if I've finally pushed the man too far. My gun is still lying in the dirt, feet away. I wait for him to hurt me, to agree with my statement, degrade me further, but he doesn't. He smooths my hair, running his fingers gently through the strands, and says, "Thank you for agreeing to see Valkarra."

He leaves me in the woods, staring after him, frozen from pleasure and shock.

CHAPTER SEVEN
Kethi

My fist slams into the rock, sending chips spraying across the ground. I can hear my brother laughing, feel Kano's smug smile, taste *her* on my lips. I send my other fist slamming into the rock.

The mountains in Valkarra are lush and green. The plants crawl and cling to their sides, acting as a cushion when you hit them. The mountains of Wupeso don't share this trait. They are hard and sharp beneath my fists. They make my knuckles bleed even through my *jisa* – which is working now that I've seen and touched my *ĝha*. More shards of rock crumble against the ground with my grunt.

Who have I become?

"You've defeated it," Liro chuckles, seeing the small hole I've smashed into the rock. It does not seem deep enough because I still do not feel like myself.

My parents prepared me to become Rogeshu from the moment my marks appeared in my youth. They taught me about Wupeso and the differences between it and Valkarra. They taught me about geography, culture, and diplomacy from a young age. I learned to push my desires aside for my people and lead by example. They built my confidence and encouraged me to trust myself and the words of Baso Sheva. So, to have my weaknesses exploited by a woman, to lose control of my mind, was unacceptable.

I dust the grit from my knuckles, watching my hands shake. The encounter on the floating island was infuriating. My *ĝha* was infuriating. She was like sunlight, bright and illuminating. She dragged me out of the darkness I hadn't even known I'd been feeling. From the moment I saw her this morning, everything felt right again. I wanted to see her, touch her, heal her. Yet, she *ran* from me, which was the most concerning fact.

My Roxie was a fighter. She was not afraid – not when she landed on this planet, not when she met me for the first time, and especially not when I caught her. It had been a bit of a thrill for me, but when she fought me – I went too far. I was no longer myself in the moment. I had merely gone after her to speak about the travel plans. I wanted to see if she was feeling better and thank her for agreeing to come to Valkarra. I needed to know that she was okay and did not hate me.

Her cold words echo in my ears.

"It's fine. It's not like it meant anything."

It had meant a lot to me. Roxie, my *ĝha*, meant everything to me. I didn't expect she would immediately feel the same. I was merely hopeful she would give me a chance. So, her words were like an icy blade through my hearts.

Unfortunately, there is work to do. I set aside her hurtful words and turned to my brother. Kano stands at his back, silent but cheery at my pitiful display. When I'd emerged from the woods and reunited with them, it was clear what had happened. Rejection did not look good on me. It was entertaining to them, however.

"You will ride ahead and prepare Valkarra for their arrival. I want a celebration in their honor. Let the *zhushe* know of their travel plans to Wupeso. I want them here by the time we touch ground in Valkarra with the human women. That includes Xatsoe."

"She will not be happy, brother," Liro says, though he is already walking toward his mount.

"Which is why you, the *kind* brother, will be the one to tell her." I said in a tone which allowed no argument.

Liro nods, his dark hair spilling forward slightly. "Yes, Rogeshu."

Mere moons ago, Kano had been begging to meet my sister Xatsoe. He wanted to meet all our *zhushe* but especially my sister. I understood his reasoning why. Her station was appealing and she had a mind of her own. Since it would not have been a love match, her wandering would have been perfect for our allied Rogeshu. Now, having met his *ĝha*, Vera, he would have been highly disappointed. Xatsoe was a fighter like Roxie, and she wore her emotions boldly, unabashed, unashamed. She, like all strong *V`òllø* women, did not care much for the wills of men and chose exploration and world study over everything else. Her beauty wasn't to be overlooked either, but Xatsoe did. Often. She found ways to make her appearance more manageable – cutting her hair short, wearing inappropriate clothing, and wearing boots with her skirts. Kano had wanted to meet her, but they would have been a terrible match.

At least I averted one crisis.

"I appreciate your expediency, Kethi Rogeshu," Kano says, wrenching me from my thoughts. I put on my placating smile and tilt my horns to the right in agreement. I was not the kind of man who did anything by halves.

"Of course. I am glad we could come to an agreement." I mean it to be gracious, but it comes off condescending, and I wince internally. I am about to dismiss myself, but Kano has more to say.

"Would you like some advice? One *ĝha* to another?"

My curiosity gets the best of me, and I tilt my horns again.

Kano is silent for so long; I expect, in his age, he's forgotten his point, but he says, "The human women need careful care. They are skeptical from their experience of men and non-human beings, and your *ĝha* has experienced more darkness than most. If you can make her feel safe, she will learn to love you much faster."

"My *ĝha* is safe. She does not fear anything with her tiny weapon," I reply without thought. I resent his words of my *ĝha*. She is strong and too bright for this 'darkness' to touch her.

"It is advice, Kethi. You may use it or not. Your choice," Kano knocks his horn with mine in a friendly gesture and turns away from me. "I hope you choose to see my wisdom."

CHAPTER EIGHT
Roxie

The battle is upon me. I refuse to lose. I make my bed at the *peholoe* loft, like my unit leader planned to check it. I donned my human uniform, forgoing the usual Wupeson style. I piled my hair into a clean bun and wrapped my belongings with a blanket and two leather straps. Had I caved under Aston's unspoken threats yesterday? Yes. Was I going to Valkarra now, after I swore I wouldn't? Also, yes. Did it mean my 'soulmate' had won? No. Absolutely not.

Operation Alien Bride was a no-go on my end. I would find a way out of this, even if I had to break this newfound bond and escape this planet. Closing my eyes, I try to still my mind, building the mental blockades I'll need to survive this plan.

"Thinking of me?"

My gun is drawn and pointed in seconds until I realize it is only Rihu taunting me. He does not react as a human would, instead gently leaning against the door and perusing my tiny room. Looking at my gun in my hands, I slide it back into my holster, ignoring the frantic beat of my heart. It seems my reaction still works – but not on the man I wanted it to.

"Nope, your bestie. He's much sexier than you," I taunt, double-checking the straps on my bag before lifting it over my shoulders. It's not necessarily the truth – if you didn't spend much time with them, you probably couldn't tell the difference between the two. But, I could, and if I had to pick, Rihu was sexier because he was slightly more pretty-boy. He was always confident and perfectly manicured. Rihu heaves the pack from my back.

"Do not lie to me, Roxie. Manipulation is not for you."

I try to tug my pack out of his hands, but he slings it over his shoulder before turning and heading toward the floating island.

"What are you doing?" I ask, following him out of the *peholoe* loft and toward our destination.

"I have been told to help you find your way. It seems your *ĝha* did not want you to get lost."

"Give me my pack," I demand, trying to process his words. It doesn't make sense for Kethi to send either of the twins. From the few interactions I've observed them have, Kethi and the twins are like fire and ice. They do not get along in the least. Plus, Kethi has a habit of surprising me when I don't want him to.

"I will carry it for you, Roxie. This is a kind human gesture, I am told."

With my bag slung over his shoulder, it is feet out of my reach. I won't succumb to my urge to jump for it. This forces me to march behind him while he holds my pack hostage. When we arrive at the floating island, I'm not surprised Kethi is not there, and Royi is. Lari is already harnessed and ready for a day's flight. Rihu's beast is prepared beside her. Royi is the one to tell me what's going on.

"If you still do not want to go to Valkarra, this is your last chance to say. We will put you in hiding until the women are gone."

I look at the beasts, saddled with their weapons and harnesses. They are prepared to stay with me for multiple days to avoid my *ĝha*.

"Why?"

"Az-ton held guilt for tricking you into volunteering. She arranged this with us last night."

Great. I can understand why Aston would do this. Since her *ĝha* believed she spent too much time with the twins, she made a point of doing so. They were more than happy to please any human that paid a lick of attention to them – both eager to have a *ĝha* of their own. And since no marks appeared, they both doted on all the human females. Aston included. So, of course, they agreed to another one of her wicked schemes. It was, yet again, brilliant and evil.

I cursed myself for knowing I would say no. Aston's best friend, Vera, was a runner. She ran from her problems, mentally and physically. She would take this offer. But I was not Vera. I was a fighter. I stood my ground and became a problem for everyone around me.

"Thank you for the offer, but I have a better plan," I reply, holding out my hand for my pack. Rihu's brows crinkle, but he hands me the sack, looking to his mount.

"What will you do?" Royi asks.

"What I've always done," I strap my pack to my shoulders. "Survive."

CHAPTER NINE
Roxie

Instead of running, I take the opportunity to get one final lesson from Royi on navigating the *uhichi*. This time, when I slide off Lari's back and begin to free fall, there is no fear. I whistle the tune Royi taught me, and Lari easily scoops me from the air. She glides along the air, careful not to jostle me as we swoop back toward the island. With careful landing, she deposits me on the edge, and I beam.

Most days on Shojo, I felt off. It wasn't depression, but life didn't hold the same meaning here. On Earth, I was a protector and provider. I had a great job that helped support my family. I was a decorated veteran. To be a soldier in a place of peace felt wrong. The most challenging day was the day of Vera's *r̈ ůṣad'ù*. That day we would have returned to Earth if the journey had been safe and the *SS Herculean* never fell victim to slaughter. Nothing seemed real. So, I counted my bullets to convince myself our new life was real. I had to use those to escape. I had to use those bullets to live.

In my moment of freefall, I didn't need to count bullets to know this life was real. I was real, and I was alive in the truest sense of the word. My blood was pumping, my muscles jellified, and my smile beaming.

I stumble forward from the ledge, closing my eyes and spinning in a circle with my head tilted toward the sky. I can hear the twins chuckling, and Lari trills her own approvals. I bump into one of the men, and an embarrassed giggle works its way out of me. I open my eyes, stumbling back a few steps. My body goes rigid.

Kethi's eyes are wide as he stares down at me. My smile is frozen on my face.

"Sunshine," He rasps, his eyes scanning my features as if he needs to commit them to memory. My smile falls, and I look around us. The twins are stifling their laughs, half-hiding behind their mounts at my surprise. The other women are walking up the trail toward the flight landing. Kethi's arms reach for me, and I take two solid steps away, rotating my shoulders back and tilting my chin down.

"Kethi," I say in a tone reserved for my leaders in the military. His eyes seem to narrow at this, but his own shoulders stiffen as he remembers himself.

"You will ride with me on my mount," He declares, motioning for his advisor to prepare his beast. I look at the twins and their mounts, especially Lari.

"Actually, Rihu and Royi have been teaching me to fly my own beast. I will be borrowing Lari for the journey. They trained her to return to this island without a rider."

I glance at Royi long enough to see his nostrils flare. We never spoke of anything, and he was attached to Lari. His horns tilt slightly to the left, and I can feel heat gather along my collarbones. My rash had been getting better over the last day, but at my insistence to spend time away from Kethi, it itched once again beneath my jumpsuit. At least he couldn't see it.

"This is unacceptable. You are my *ĝha*; you ride my beast. Not the mount of another man." In this statement, he sounds like a king. Like the first night I met him, his confidence and boldness led him. He is confident this is the way he would like to move forward. But I was crushing Operation Alien Bride.

Aston shows up behind me. Her wild hair bounces as she glances between me and Kethi. Erja must have decided to join us last minute because she arrived just behind her with Ian in tow. *Five teammates. Well, four and a half.*

"Is something wrong here?" Aston asks, relaxing the tension with her cheery tone.

"Roxie will be riding with me," Kethi says, "There is nothing wrong."

With a tight smile and a huff of breath, I respond, "I will be riding Lari, so I can practice my flight skills."

Aston weighs both of our statements, the gears in her mind turning. With each passing day, I swear she becomes more and more like the Aston she must have been on Earth. She accessorizes more, organizes schedules between the women, and leads the human council. It's like night and day between when I met her and now. Formerly, she was a quivering mess, clinging to Vera like she'd drift into the vast abyss of space if she didn't. Now, she made secret plans on my behalf and butted in to defend me against my own *ĝha*.

My own *ĝha*. A shiver worked its way down my back at the thought before my mind forcefully replaced it with Kethi Rogeshu. Unfortunately, his name was not much better to stomach, reminding me of his husky voice in the woods yesterday.

"Oh, I'm sorry, Kethi Rogeshu," Aston starts, "I'm terrified of heights, so I was hoping to ride with Roxie on a mount I know. The twins said it would be okay as long as they could ride together and meet us in Valkarra. Of course, they won't be staying, only acting as an escort for my comfort."

Kethi's jaw twitched, and I wondered if he wanted to grind his teeth. Telling me no was one choice; risking the entire human visitation over sharing a mount with his *ĝha* was another. I could see how quick he made new calculations, moving the pieces around the board like an expert player. His polite smile tilted his lips, revealing the tiny points of his fangs. Somehow, they made him seem more approachable.

"I'd already planned for your fears, Az-ton. My own brother, a skilled flier, will be flying you. Kano needs Rihu and Royi this morning."

Aston could tell he caught her in her lie, but she didn't cave or show embarrassment. I couldn't explain how grateful I was for her. Or how incredible it was to have her on my side. I watch her carefully and can see when she decides to cede this argument. She was honest about her fears, and her idea had been sound, but it didn't work. So, rather than start a political nightmare, she nods appreciatively.

"Wow, how generous of you and your family. Where is your brother?"

"Liro," He calls, waving over a man who looks nothing like him. The only characteristic they have in common is they're both blue, but it's not even the same shade. This Liro character looks much smaller than Kano, but I imagine he is fast. And the first time I met him, they introduced him as an advisor, not Kethi's brother.

"Rogeshu," Liro taps Kethi's horns in deference. Kethi motions to Aston, who smiles like a predator in his direction.

"This is Az-ton An-droos. She is Llazho's *ĝha* and an important visitor to Valkarra. She will be riding with you, and I expect you to treat her with the utmost care."

Aston's eyes dim at her introduction as Llazho's *ĝha*, and I can only imagine the slurry of thoughts going through her head. From our morning conversations, I learned Aston had been quite the bigshot on Earth. A prominent gallerist, artist, and brand for high-value art and artistic talent, she had built a new name for herself even though her father owned an empire of his own that she would inherit billions of. I realize she's been my teammate in this operation, and she's been doing all the protection.

"Actually, Aston is her own person. On Earth, she was Aston Andrews, phenomenal artist and leader of a large art company."

"You like art?" Liro asks, his alien eyes flickering full to narrow.

"No. I love art. I miss art. I used to eat, sleep, and breathe art," She explains, stepping away with Liro and tossing me an apologetic smile. I trail them with my eyes the entire way to Liro's mount. He leans in and listens well to what she has to say, showing her genuine connection, without any mention of her *ĝha* since we got here. When I can't hear them anymore, I turn back to Kethi. His eyes are on mine.

"Since you do not have to escort Miss Az-ton, you can ride with me."

The unhealed teen in me wants to whine, "Oh, I can, can I?" But I don't go there. I slide my tongue across my top teeth, making a sucking noise my mother would have reprimanded me for.

"I would prefer to ride alone." I keep my arms crossed in front of me and pretend the degree it tilted my neck is a natural angle that doesn't bother me.

"Oh, Sunshine, your preferences stopped mattering when you got sick."

Arrogant ass. I was shocked that Kethi didn't sling me over his shoulder like a caveman. With the way he treated me in the forest – No. I don't allow myself to think about the forest because as much as I hated my weakness afterward, I would not taint the memory with regret. I had enough regret to last me a lifetime. It surprised me when he didn't mishandle me further. But I had a plan. I needed to stick to it.

"How did you know?" I demand.

"I have my ways."

I do what he apparently does best, negotiate. "If you tell me 'your ways,' I will ride with you to Valkarra without further complaint."

He seems to consider my proposal, not immediately responding to my demands. When he decided this was a fair trade, he confirmed what I already knew.

"I sent Liro to check on you when my *jisa* stopped working."

I press my lips together, keeping my desire to comfort him or ask further questions to myself.

"Which mount is yours?" I ask instead, keeping my composure. He points to an *uhichi* with a stark white beak. "It's name?"

"His name is *Nyu-zho*," He tells me. My hand wraps around one of the carrying straps of my pack, and he follows suit. I try only once to tug it from his grip, and when he doesn't let up, I drop my hand like it's on fire.

"*Nyuzho*," I repeat, testing the unfamiliar word on my tongue. My translation bud says it's something akin to 'divine wish.' It sounds like a difficult name to live up to, and I wonder if Nyuzho feels the same way I do about being bound to Kethi Rogeshu.

He straps my pack to the bird, and I run the back of my hand down its oily feathers. Nyuzho is not much different than Lari, a bit wider in his chest, definitely taller. He has a scar across his left wing and doesn't jump or ruffle when I walk beneath his neck. He's perched closer to the edge than Lari, and I wonder if Kethi commanded him to be here or if he likes feeling the breeze on his tail feathers. *Does he know the same commands?*

I tentatively do the heel whistle and watch Lari perk up, but Nyuzho ignores me. Rihu and Royi aren't messing with their mounts, just talking with the other Valkarran visitors who arrived here to help escort us to Valkarra overnight. But it also means their mounts are unattended.

"Hey, Kethi," I say, waiting for him to look at me over his mount. His eyes seem to sear into mine, and I must calm my beating heart to stick with my plan.

"Yes, Sunshine?"

"Do you think Nyuzho can catch me faster than Lari?" I ask before tossing myself over the ledge for the second time this morning. The same rush of adrenaline, the feeling of being alive invades me. I wait an entire Mississippi before I start the whistle to call for Lari. I can see Kethi's eyes as he leans over the edge. The color is blown wide, dark blue eating up the almond-shaped space; his mouth drops open in disbelief. My lips purse to whistle, and I flip him both middle fingers.

Lari snatches me out of the air, and I can't help but tilt my head beneath her claws and feel the air brush across the back of my neck. I click for her to bank right and direct her to land at an entirely different floating island. I technically wasn't breaking my promise not to complain, but I never said anything about being easy to manage. If he wanted me to ride with him, he could come find me here and strap me to his mount himself.

CHAPTER TEN
Kethi

I should have expected a stunt from my *ĝha*. When I arrived, I was so enraptured by her smile that I forgot she made nothing easy for me. At the moment, she had been sunshine, bright and enticing. I wanted to bathe in her glory and feel her warmth. Instead, she argued about riding with me, though she had no idea where she was going and less than a month of training with the *uhichi*. Her friend, *Az-ton*, almost had me convinced of her little stunt, and I was moments from letting her get away with her lies, too, until I saw Royi shaking his horns. Worst of all, I hated to decide on the spot, and with Roxie, I seemed to do nothing else.

They trained me to make decisions under pressure, but being backed into a corner was still foreign to me nonetheless. I worked tirelessly to ensure Valkarra made their negotiations from a place of strength. My own choices were one way to strengthen my city or my family further. So, to have my *ĝha*, of all people, turn me on my head was difficult.

With Nyuzho flying like the wind, I found her sitting on the ledge of a floating island across the lands. She had a flower in her hand and a smile on her face, and I wondered what she thought. Maybe of her home? Family? The tiny metal pieces in her weapon?

Nyuzho caws at our arrival, and Roxie's head snaps up. She stands back from the ledge to give Nyuzho space to pass. He does. I motion for her to get on, and she glares in my direction. Carefully, she approaches Nyuzho, and I see the issue. My *ĝha* is very small.

I dismount, standing in front of her for what feels like an entire sliver of the sun. Does she even want my help? Will she let me touch her? Her preferences don't matter at this moment because I can see the other human women are already leaving the edge of the floating island, beginning their trek to Valkarra.

"I can't mount him on my own. He's even bigger than Lari," She says, eyeing the looped seats. I only nod.

I use her hand to tug her closer and feel my *jisa* strengthen at the touch. A tiny sliver of her silky black hair has slipped from the knot at the back of her head. With a gentle finger, I slide it behind her ear. A stifled whimper leaves her lips. Ignoring the shot of vitality in my bones, I step behind her, placing my hands on her tiny hips. Roxie is small but sturdy; still, my hands almost wrap her tiny waist. I feel her shiver under my touch, and masculine satisfaction buckles through me. I grip her hips a little bit and lift her slight weight into the loops of the front seat. I keep her steady with a hand on her back as she tightens the loops around her thighs, checking her weapon is also securely attached.

When my hands lift from her body, they tingle with pleasure, and I want to put them back. I want to use them to roam across her bare skin, pull her thighs apart, and –

"Are we going?"

I clear my thoughts, shaking out my hands before climbing up behind her. She sits up straight, trying to keep her back from relaxing into mine. I can see the tension in her body, and I ache to ease it. But before I can overthink it, I whistle a quiet combination, and Nyuzho takes us home.

CHAPTER ELEVEN
Roxie

Even from the sky, you can tell Wupeso and Valkarra are different. Valkarra is so green. Surrounded by mountains, water cuts through the village, turning into a pond near its center. As Nyuzho sweeps around the small island, the smell of moss and river fills the air. The mount swings down low along the edge of the mountain, and I see an animal with horns spook, scurrying away into the woods.

Even the trees are different. In Wupeso, they're dark, spindly, jungle-style trees that droop low and support the other underbrush. They have multiple layers of tree covers, with the canopy far above and thick enough to keep a dark mist inside. Here, they're more like pines. Instead of leaves, there are colorful little spines so dark green they're almost black. Instead of spiky cones, they spread out wide at the top, tiny branches curving back beneath to support the larger ones. And off the trunks, bright pink mushrooms sprout from the rough silver bark. Beds of salmon and sage-colored moss cushion the ground and climb the rough edges of rock.

Nyuzho comes to perch along a manmade stone balconette. A small stream of water trickles through the brush off to the side. Some of the trees grow out of the shale-like mountainside.

Kethi helps me down without a word, turning back to Nyuzho to get him unstrapped. I take the chance to look around. The other human women are all congregated by a massive cave entrance, listening animatedly to whatever wild story Aston is telling them. The other *uhichi* are being tended to by Valkarran men. Even they appear different.

The men in Wupeso are gruff. They take good care of themselves, they're clean, they wear nice clothes, but here the men are groomed, spotless, and tailored. I should have expected this since Kethi is always picture-perfect. But it's more than the way they present themselves. Their weave is finer, the men wear jeweled cuffs around their upper arms, their shoes are shinier. And they have more women. The morale was so much better because women were given. Many of these men had *V`òllø* wives who stood by gratefully and watched because they had returned too.

Back in Wupeso, the *peholoe* were exacting and intimidating because only two months before I arrived, they thought their village would die out. Even then, you couldn't deny the beauty of the women. Hoga was stunning with her icy blue countenance. Gowi and Rra looked like Amazonian warriors meant to blend into the greens of the jungle. Even Pa was handsome. A silver fox, Alba had called him under the influence of *tsare* one night.

But none of them had the beauty of youth on their side, unlike the *V`òllø* woman swiftly coming my way. My hand itched to reach for my gun, but no one seemed concerned enough to stop her, so I hoped she was friendly. She was tall and lengthy. She strutted like a supermodel, letting her long white braids swing behind her. Her horns were tall and curly, and she wound tiny metal beads around them, which glinted in the evening sun.

Meanwhile, I was saddle sore. My thighs and butt ached from the ride, and even my back gave me trouble because I had refused to lean against Kethi. Oh, my god. Kethi. I look at the *V`òllø* female again, my eyes dashing around her features, checking off the boxes. She looked like a feminine version of him. Curvaceous, instead of blocky, soft eyes with bright lashes framing them, the dress with slits for her long, shapely legs. Instead of icy blue skin, hers was amethyst, but the pointy fangs remained. Even her smile was like a carbon copy. Who was I about to meet? His mother? A sister? Some cousin or aunt? Before I could prepare for the worst, the woman pointed her horns down at me and charged.

Oh shit. Oh, shit. Oh, shit. I squeeze my eyes closed and feel her horns whiz past my face. Hot, oddly floral breath huffs across my face, and I hear a little giggle.

"Tangle with my horns," She says in her language, her eyes brought down to my level. Carefully, I reach my hands up and wrap them around her horns, feeling the metallic beads press into my palms. After a few moments, she says, "Now, let go."

I drop my hands to my sides, watching her stand to her full height. From a distance, I thought she was taller than Kethi, but I can see now she is not. Instead of coming to her chest, like I do with him, I come right below her chin. She tilts her horns back, looking down her nose at me curiously.

"So, you are Roxie, the hyu-man," She says, leaning back down to peer closer at my eyes.

"Sure am," I answer carefully, feeling odd under her scrutiny. She seemed to figure out what she wanted to know about my eyes and stood straight.

"Wonderful to meet you. I'm Xatsoe, Kethi's favorite sister," She tosses a collection of braids back over her shoulder, peering behind me to keep an eye on her brother. She seemed confident, but when she caught sight of Kethi, she got jittery. "Do you want to walk into town with me?"

She doesn't give me a chance to respond before her hand grabs mine like a child, and she starts down the trail at a break-neck pace. I'm in a comfortable jog to keep up with her, and she keeps glancing over her shoulder as if we're running from the police.

"Is everything okay?" I ask, tugging my hand from hers while keeping pace.

"Oh, yeah. Everything is Sheva blessed," She replies, going a tinge faster and forcing me to meet her jog.

"Is there a reason we're running?" I ask, feeling my thighs burning. I had already exhausted them from the ride, and now pushing them forward to jog downhill had me reaching my limits.

"We're not running," She huffs, "Merely walking with purpose."

"And that purpose is?"

"Escaping my brother, so we can have some proper sisterly time before he ships me off to Wupeso to bond to that beast Kano."

My confusion skyrockets, but I continue to keep pace, "Kano is already married."

She stops in her tracks, "What?"

"Kano married a human woman named Vera like a month ago."

"They had a *r ̈ u̥ṣad'ù*?" She asks disbelief in her tone. I can hear the chatter of the other women on the trail behind us, and I nod.

"Oh, Thank Baso Sheva." She breathes, placing both her hands over her hearts. She begins back down the hill much slower, and I walk with her, wondering what we will chat about now. "Are you tired? Would you like to bathe?"

"Warm water sounds like heaven," I admit. Her brow crinkles, but she leads me to a massive stucco building and in through frosted doors. Inside, it's like a fancy lobby. Another female *V`òllø* sits at a counter beside a jug of water and two wooden cups. Colorful woven cushions surround a tiny table, and the runic language is burned into waxy leaves.

"Hey Luxelle, this is Roxie. We're going to the bathhouse for a soak."

Luxelle barely looks up from her Neked'I chips, tilting her horns to the right in acquiescence. So, Xatsoe leads me through a hallway and into a much larger bathhouse. It makes the one in the *peholoe* loft look like a child's tub. Hot water steams in a massive oval pool with a teal and white mosaic across the bottom. Some nude *V`òllø* women chat in a circle on the far end, and Xatsoe doesn't hesitate to join them.

Standing beside a small wooden stool, she strips out of her dress, leaving some of her jewelry stacked atop her outfit to avoid getting it wet. Then, she walks down the steps without me, greeting the other women.

Halfway across the pool, she asks, "You coming?"

I hurry to join them, leaving my human clothes crumpled on the floor beside hers and leaving my bra and underwear on.

I step onto the first step of the pool and feel the familiar, comforting burn of the warm water on my skin. My already rosy tint reddens further, and the parts of me beneath the water begin looking like cooked lobster as I slowly work my way across the pool.

Xatsoe is in a deep conversation with the other women, but they still rejoice when I join them. The happy exclamations one might expect from their mother and her friends begin as I'm introduced.

"This is Roxie. My dull-headed brother finally decided to bring her to Valkarra."

They all coo over me, inspecting my face and features curiously. When one of them stares at my hip, I cover it with my hand, and a flush rushes to my cheeks. My tattoo was for me and me only. It was a choice I made to remind myself not to take life too seriously. Her perusal of my body didn't stop, but nothing else felt quite as intrusive, even as her eyes locked on the juncture of my thighs.

"So, Roxie," One of the other women began. Her belly was slightly rounded, and she had curly lilac hair against similarly colored skin. "Tell us about your home."

"Earth is home to eight-billion humans and a variety of ecosystems," I begin, spouting the information from the planetarium video on board the *SS Herculean*. I don't get too far before Xatsoe interrupts.

"Sounds dreadfully boring. Tell us about *your* home. What was your dwelling like? Do you have a family?"

"Oh," I say, a wave of sadness brushing through me. Since being on Shojo, I have done my best to avoid thoughts of home. Aside from my early mornings on the floating island, I didn't give myself space to think of my family. And even when I did, it ended in me worrying about Satine and my mother. I would wonder if they were okay, if they missed me. I would wonder if my mother would cry or if she thought I'd had enough of her nagging and blamed herself for my disappearance. We both knew we loved one another even if we rarely saw eye-to-eye.

"Look what you've gone and done, Xattie," One of the women reprimands. I can feel my eyes watering, and I blink back my tears, trying to conjure the sound of my drill sergeant in my head asking me if I wanted him to give me something to cry about.

"It's fine," I half-choke. "I have a sister, and my parents are still alive. My father is from America, where I grew up. My mother met him in Japan, a different place. When he was visiting, they fell in love in three days. She immigrated to be with him, and when everything was copacetic with the government, they had my sister, Satine. Two years later, me. My mother loved musical films."

"What is a *government*?" One of the women asks, slaughtering the word. I'm happy to answer this question because it's much less personal.

"It's a country's leadership. Kethi would be your government because he leads this village and decides how you interact with other villages. Kano does the same for Wupeso, it seems."

The stab of impending tears recedes, and the women nod in understanding. I use the silence to turn the tables.

"So, are you women single, or do you have mates?"

They seem scandalized by my words, and I have to wonder what I've done wrong. They're all sitting with their legs crossed in the water, but even I know the familiar glow of a *ĝha* tattoo. Looking around, I notice everyone, but Xatsoe, has one.

"They all have *ĝhajo,*" Xatsoe answers for them, glancing uncomfortably between them.

"Did I say something wrong?" I ask, the discomfort in my chest growing. I felt a heaviness weigh on me, and I decided visiting the bathhouse had been a terrible idea. I should have waited for Kethi. I don't even know Xatsoe.

Xatsoe tries to explain, "Mate is a hurtful word because mates are unblessed by Baso Sheva. Also, when you do not have a *ĝha*, you are a *zhushe*. I feel it is a mistranslation, this word *single.*"

I want to groan. Instead, I apologize. "I'm tired from the travel. Can we try again another time?"

The women all tilt their horns to the right, and I hurry out of the pool. I'm dressed, and my hair is dripping down my back when I realize I have no idea where I'm going. Xatsoe did not get out of the pool with me, and I was standing in the lobby of the bathhouse ten seconds from hyperventilating. I've only been in Valkarra for a single hour, and I'm already ruining it.

Stepping outside the doors, I feel a comforting breeze carry the smell of river water to me. I lean against one of the bathhouse pillars and close my eyes. *What to do? What to do?*

I sink to the ground against the pillar and draw my gun from my holster. I click the release for my magazine and roll the top bullet in its spot, counting the casings inside. I pry one out of the chamber and slide it to the top of the magazine before shoving it back into the gun and racking it. I still tucked the full magazine into the slot beside my holster. I mentally count my bullets again, landing on sixteen total, and put my gun back in place.

All my energy subsequently leaves my body.

I don't know where the other human women are, and I have no interest in trekking back up the hill to check there. Valkarra is busier than Wupeso, and the people are packed into a smaller stretch of land. From the entrance to the bathhouse, I can see dozens of stucco homes stacked atop one another like apartment buildings and multifamily dwellings. People walk the streets with tiny *V`òllø* children skipping around beside them. There must be a public market or something nearby because the sound of *V`òllø* voices carries on the breeze, providing the same ambiance of a busy city.

A gust of wind blows through, and dust flies from the packed dirt, blowing into my still-wet hair. *Great.* I stand up and dust myself off, preparing to give myself a tour of Valkarra, when Xatsoe comes slipping out of the bathhouse with the women laughing.

"Oh, you're still here," She breezes as if she didn't let me make a fool of myself and then stay with her girls when I had to leave.

To make matters worse, I hear Kethi's shout, "Xatsoe Dzi˘llo˘súhì, you better have a good reason for still being in Valkarra and to steal my *ĝha* no less."

Kethi looks angry. His brows are drawn low, his eye color has overtaken his eyes, he crosses his arms tightly over his chest, and he stares down at his sister. I keep myself pressed against the wall and ignore the continued feeling of being out of place. Xatsoe doesn't bother to act reprimanded, instead twirling one of her braids between her fingers.

"Oh, please. I was introducing *your ĝha* to the women of the city. It's not like you were going to."

Kethi fumes, and I watch his fists clench at his sides. I want to rub his shoulders and apologize for sneaking off without him. I want his tension to ease because I feel bad about causing any part of it. His sister, who I'm realizing is as bad as I expected, doesn't care if she might be giving him an aneurysm. She pushes his buttons.

"You should be in Wupeso by now, Princess."

"And you should be pumping your *ĝha* full of new life, but it looks like neither of us is living up to expectations today."

My distaste for his sister grows by the minute, and my hands itch to grab my gun. I wouldn't shoot anyone for being a bitch (necessarily), but a low level of rage starts when I see her disrespect him.

"You're going to Wupeso," Kethi says with finality. Xatsoe flashes her eyes in his direction, which I expect is similar to an eye roll.

"Don't expect me to come back married," She spits. With a stomp, she and the women head off toward the landing cliff, presumably to do as the Rogeshu says.

I am pleased his sister is gone. Some of my frustration drains out until he turns his eyes on me.

"Don't run off like that."

Disbelief courses through my veins. I survived before Kethi, and I would survive after. Before he forced me to come here, he had been all prince charming, trying to convince me to visit with his sweets and smiles. Apparently, now, I'd given him too much trouble. He didn't try diplomacy first. He jumped straight to intimidation and demands.

"I was with your sister. And you didn't brief me properly. You trust family – Liro is your advisor. You were busy, and I made an executive decision."

He presses me against the column, bringing his forehead to mine.

"And when was I supposed to brief you, Sunshine? When you were running through the woods, avoiding me? When you were fighting about riding arrangements? When you were tossing yourself off a ledge to spite me? Tell me when I had the time."

His words are hard, but his hand on my side is gentle. He rubs circles under my shirt against my bare skin, making it buzz. The reminder of the woods has me melting beneath his touch even though the rest of my actions bring me shame. Kethi wasn't wrong, and that was the most infuriating situation yet. I hadn't figured him out, and my plan to avoid being the next alien bride required intimate knowledge of him.

It tastes like acid, but I say it.

"I'm sorry."

His eye color widens slightly, and I can tell I've surprised him. The truth is, I'm tired. From the moment I landed on this planet and didn't get torn apart by one of these guys, I've been tired. It's like I had been running on adrenaline from when the ship sirens started blaring to when I felt any sort of safety. Eventually, once I was safe, I stopped. When I sleep, I'm in the same adrenaline-fueled nightmare; when I'm awake, I'm exhausted.

I expect Kethi to double down on his reprimand, blaming me and telling me I should do better. It's what my mother would do, what Kano would have done. I expect he will ask me to repent or something or use it to his advantage and press for something he wants from me. He doesn't.

He stands back and says, "Apology accepted. We will forget this ever happened."

"Okay. Good." I say, forcing myself to trust his words. Kethi only lied by omission, so I figured I had to trust he meant what he said. "Now, can you show me where the human women stay?"

My shoulders droop, and his brows furrow once more. "You're not staying with the human women. You're staying with me."

CHAPTER TWELVE
Kethi

My Sunshine is a fighter. This is good in times of war, but we are not at war. We are in loving peace. Still, she fights me every step of our way.

"I'm not staying with you," She rebuts, crossing her arms over her chest. Her jumpsuit is wrinkled, and her hair is wet, and all I want to do is get her into clean, dry clothes and hold her in my bed. After a moon cycle apart and the infamous soul sickness wracking our bodies, I figured this would be an obvious choice. The closer we stay together, the better for the both of us.

"It will help you feel better," I tell her, trying my best to be diplomatic even though every fiber of my being is telling me to throw the tiny woman over my shoulder and carry her home like a *yàḥàḥo*.

"I feel fine."

"But you could feel fantastic."

"I've felt what you can do, and 'fantastic' is a bit of a stretch," She spits, glaring into my eyes. Her eyes are odd. Dark, dark brown circles surround a black pupil, and the mass of circles moves around in its socket as she looks from place to place. But I liked them because they tell me when she lies to me. They twitch with her mistruths, and when her mind wanders to what we did in the woods, they widen at the memory.

"Would you like me to try again?" I offer, feeling roguish.

Her cheeks heat a beautiful red color I adore, and her face snaps away. She tries to look at anything except me. Unfortunately for her, I have her caged against the column of the bathhouse. Her eyes meet my bicep, trail the muscles of my arm and move to my chest. My marks are glowing under her perusal. I wish she would follow her eyes with her hands. Unfortunately, her eyes close, and she ignores me, dropping her chin to her chest. When they snap back to meet mine, she fills them with anger, and small pleasure moves through me at the sight. This is Roxie. This is My Sunshine.

"We won't be trying anything again. Now show me where the human women are staying."

I remind myself I can't act like a barbarian whenever she defies me. *Ĝhajo* were worth more than lovers, and as such, they deserved to see the truest parts of their equal match. I could be the best version of myself for her. I could show her my tact and diplomacy.

"What if we were to make a deal?" I ask, watching the spark behind her eye.

"I'm not like Vera; I won't gamble away my freedom. Take me to the other women."

I know she's not like Vera. I did not want Vera. "It is not a gamble but an exchange."

"I have nothing to give you."

"Yet you hold everything I want," It's a bold reply, but I stand by it.

"You can't have me."

"How about your acquiescence?"

"You mean my submission."

"No, Sunshine. Submission would suggest I'm superior in some way. We both know that's not true. So, humor me. Ask about the deal."

I watch her consider my offer, calculating how bad of an idea it might be. But eventually, she asks, "What is your deal?"

"You can stay with the human women at night if you spend your days with me. Or you can spend your days among the human women, but you spend your nights with me. I get something I want, and you get something you want."

The Baso Sheva would curse me for the things I was willing to give to have her in my bed, but further, they would smite me for the tantalizing option of spending every waking hour in her presence. There were so many things I wanted to experience with her, share with her, and show her. Somehow, Baso Sheva softened her enough to deliver her to my village, and now it was up to me to keep her here. Before Roxie, it felt like I was in eternal darkness, untethered. With Sunshine around, everything seemed brighter and more effortless.

"Are nights like sundown to sunup or for sleeping or after dinner? How are we defining our terms?"

"From the final sliver of the sun to the first," I explain. She does not seem to like this, but ultimately she decides.

"This feels like no decision at all, but I will spend the nights with you," She says. The excitement begins to bubble in my chest, and my smile widens. "But, you have to show me where the human women are staying, and if you cross any boundaries, I get to stay with them."

My smile thins, "Name your boundaries."

She holds up three tiny fingers, pointing to the tip of each one as she lists off her expectations, "No romantic touches. No kissing. And *no* sex."

I'm a gentleman, so I agree to her terms. I throw her over my shoulder – like I would a child – and carry her through Valkarra even as she shouts for me to put her down.

CHAPTER THIRTEEN
Roxie

Kethi's place is a compound. When he drags me through the wooden gates woven with bluish vines, he puts me down and gives me a chance to gain my bearings. Taking a quick glance around, I catalog every entrance or exit point on the property, and there are many. There's the gate we came in and at least two others I can see from my vantage point. His home is full of them too. A white wood I haven't seen in Wupeso makes up his doors and shudders. All his windows are thrown open to let in the fresh evening air. Those doors, windows, and gates make up at least twenty-two exit routes I can find. He can't hold me prisoner here like he did during our travels.

He had walked me through town, pointing out where the women were staying, all while pushing my boundaries. He kept his hands platonically placed, and though my body didn't agree, there was nothing sexy about being jostled over the man's shoulder. I felt flustered before he set me down, but now I was aware of my surroundings. I had some semblance of control.

His hot breath is on my ear as he whispers, "Thinking of escaping?"

My eyes snap to him, and our mouths are too close together. Glancing down at his lips, heat erupts in my belly. One of his fangs tugs at his bottom lip, making me want to touch him. Ripping my eyes upwards once again, I find his pointed at me. They are blue and beautiful, and focused. Kethi is always so *focused*. He doesn't split his attention, and it's enthralling. Especially when his focus is on *me*.

I force myself to step back, making nausea roll through me. Ignoring the undignified gurgle of my stomach, I push my shoulders back.

"Just cataloging my options."

This makes Kethi smile. Graciously, he tilts his horns in agreement.

"Would you like a tour?"

I would like nothing more, but I don't want to appear too eager.

"Are you offering?"

"Of course, Sunshine. I wish for you to have all you desire."

The sincerity in his voice makes goosebumps pop up across my upper arms. I ignore the sensation and force myself to meet his eyes. My instinct is to look away, but I refuse to appear weakened by him. *Your illness already humbled you.* I push the thought from my mind.

"Lead the way, Mr. Rogeshu."

He offers his arm like a proper gentleman in a Regency film, and I try to be polite when I don't take it. He shrugs, unperturbed by my snub, and begins walking and talking. The outer courtyard, his words, not mine, is a gift from his people and a public meeting space. He points out certain shrubs and explains how they've developed over the seasons to be the strongest, most weather-resistant variety through a mix of cross-breeding and only keeping the most potent plants.

He plucks an unnaturally orange flower from a bush and offers it to me. My fingers brush his, and he releases the flower with his signature smile before spinning back toward the house and continuing on his way. Confusion spirals through me at the sense of loss I feel when he gains distance, but I don't let it control me. I hurry to catch up and listen intently as he explains the many doors.

Homes in Wupeso are generally circular. The rooms make up little half-moons, and you wind through them to reach the room you're looking for. Aside from the *peholoe* loft, this has been my experience on Shojo. Here, in Valkarra, the homes are similar to those on Earth, this one included. Save one significant difference. Most of the doors are on the outside.

His voice is reverent as he explains, "This door leads to our bedroom. It faces the sun's rising so Baso Sheva's light may bless us each morning. The bedroom is associated with fire."

We walk to the next one around the corner, and he explains further, "This is where we eat. It is associated with Shojo since our food comes from its grounds. In most homes, this is a gathering place."

"You don't eat outside like they do in Wupeso?"

"Only for large feasts and special occasions." He explains, walking along the side of the house and further into his tour. There are two more doors. The one opposite the bedroom is the bathhouse, and it's associated with water. Finally, the last one is for mediation and prayer, associated with air. He explains that his home symbolizes balance for the Rogeshu, and we've returned to door number one.

He opens it for me and scoops me into his arms.

"Not this again," I groan, expecting him to toss me over his shoulder, but he doesn't. Kethi only bands his arms tighter around my back and legs and carries me over the threshold before he sets me back down. "What was that about?"

"It is bad luck to enter the Rogeshu's home without expressed permission, so when a Rogeshu finds their *ĝha*, they carry them inside so everyone knows they are welcome there without a doubt."

"Sounds romantic," I glare. "We have a similar human custom, except it usually only happens on a wedding night."

"It is not romantic. I would not disrespect your boundaries so." He says, straightening up.

"You're really skirting the rules, huh?"

If he had a response, I didn't listen because I was too busy taking in my newest home. Or should I say, the mess? The *peholoe* loft was always spotless. Between the children's adherence to chores and Pa's anxiety cleaning, there was never a speck of dirt or a dirty cloth out of place. Shockingly, this was not the case for Kethi. His room was cluttered and disorganized. His bed lay unmade against the far wall beside a bedside table stacked high with items I knew nothing of. A woven basket acts as a hamper to my left, and half his clothes overflow from the bin. He looks anxious, doubled over to pick up the few articles of clothing he didn't even bother to shotput across the room. This was so unlike Kethi I'd learned of that I could not reconcile the man with the mess.

"You're a slob," I blurt, wrinkling my nose with distaste. My mother would have a conniption. My military leaders would have made me scrub my room with my toothbrush. And then *use* it.

"I have been a bit preoccupied," he admits. He runs a hand through his short, bright hair, and I see the blue color deepen near his horns slightly. He rests a hand on the base of his horn, and his eyes drop to the floor. When they return to me, he says, "I didn't expect you."

Since I have no self-preservation, I ask, "What do you mean?"

From how he pauses, I wonder if he's considering all the answers I've come up with. He wasn't expecting me, a human, as his mate. He wasn't expecting me, Roxie, a prickly girl with no filter. He wasn't expecting me here in his bedroom or expecting me to give in and visit his hometown. Maybe he wasn't expecting me to stay with him, even given his tantalizing deal and diplomacy.

"I didn't expect a *ĝha* at all."

Damn.

"Well, here I am. And unless we find a way to break this bond, we're stuck together."

CHAPTER FOURTEEN
Kethi

My hearts stall in my chest. Roxie said she did not want to be bonded to me. Pain and anger mingle inside me. *Stuck.* It is now my most hated word. She is my life's light, yet she feels stuck with me. As though I am *ur'e gu* on her fingers – not her *ĝha*. I feel frozen in the weight of her damnation.

"It's not as if you asked for this," she continues. As if she has not already broken my spirit. "Valkarra wasn't in dire straits like Wupeso."

The more she speaks, the more I feel my control slipping away. My *ĝha* knows nothing of Valkarra. She knows nothing of our resilience – nothing of the pain we've suffered since losing so many of our own. She knows *nothing* about what I have asked for. I may not have prayed sun-up to sun-down for a *ĝha*, but I asked for one. I wanted one as much as my next breath. A woman to spoil, to tangle with on a cold night. Of course, I wanted a *ĝha*. Of course, I wanted Roxie.

"I'm sure there were plenty of other Valkarran women you wanted over me."

Her words destroy any attempt I may have made to hide my emotions. My jaw must be on the floor with what she has said. I can feel my horns drooping forward, my brows raised in disbelief. Yet she stands carelessly, looking anywhere but me, biting her lip – hopefully to hold back more nonsense she wishes to babble. As she goes to speak further into the darkness, I gather my wits and interrupt her.

"Stop before the darkness overtakes you, Sunshine."

Her teeth clamp shut with an audible click before she begins worrying her bottom lip once again. With the forefinger on her right hand, she taps the side of her weapon's sheath, keeping her eyes forward. Roxie seems to look through me, and I wonder where her mind has gone.

When I step forward, her back straightens. Her hands come down tight to her sides, and her eyes flick to mine. She seems to barely breathe. I find her reaction unfamiliar, but I have not seen my *ĝha* in an entire moon cycle. Maybe she is more submissive than I first believed. I am immediately corrected when her eyes narrow in my direction as the tips of my toes meet hers. It seems my *ĝha* is always displeased with me, but she will not remain that way for long. Her glare will not derail me.

"My mother taught me many tales, Sunshine, yet none exceeds the story of Vova and her *ĝha*. Vova experienced heartbreak after heartbreak, always finding love, but never one so true it ached to be without it. Until she found her *ĝha*, Kisaso. For Vova, Kisaso was a revelation. For me, that revelation is you."

CHAPTER FIFTEEN
Roxie

What the hell do you say to that? My mind repeats his words like a broken record. *For me, that revelation is* you. Me? I'm no revelation. He knew about me for a month. I'm the one who got sick because he bailed on me. He's the one who was the big surprise. Before I fully comprehend my actions, I'm shoving at his chest.

"Why would you say that?" I shout, even as he doesn't budge, making me sway instead. His eyes darken, for real. Instead of the steady baby blue they've been, they become like sapphires. His deep and impenetrable gaze lands on mine, and I can see his anger. I've ruffled him for the first time since I met him. And if he thinks it will intimidate me, he has another fight coming.

Through clenched teeth, he growls, "What would you have me say?"

His anger is evident. Tension carves lines in his usually smooth face. The shimmer above his skin, the *jisa*, crackles bright like electricity along a wire. His shoulders bunch up, and the veins in his forearms pop. Yet his words are still measured – borderline diplomatic.

"Anything but that," I shout, trying to shove him again. His fingers wrap my wrists, and he walks me backward until we're both pressed against the door. Even keeping his arms at his chest, my arms are pinned above my head, and I have to crane my neck to see him.

"I will not take back my words simply because you are uncomfortable with the truth."

"I wouldn't ask you to if I believed them." I spit back, my own rage boiling beneath the surface. There were so many circumstances I was angry about back on Earth. From my family doting over my sister and ignoring my accomplishments to how the military treated me after I dedicated years of my life to their ridiculous wars. I was angry at the *SS Herculean* staff for preparing our teams for first contact, while swearing up and down we wouldn't run into any trouble. Of course, when I was finally safe and coming to terms with letting my anger go, that Shojo could be a fresh start, Kethi had to come and dredge it all up again. "If I was such a revelation, why didn't you fight harder for me?"

Kethi's nostrils flare. His hands tighten minimally on my wrists. I can see his gears turning, but he closes his eyes. He returns his composure with a deep breath. Then, his hands release me, and he steps away. He glances out the window at the darkening sky.

"You may not know this about me yet, Sunshine, but you will learn; when it comes to a fight as important as the one for your heart, I would never disgrace you by seeking immediate gratification."

The tension dissipates when he leaves me in a mess of shallow breaths against the door while he finishes tidying the room. Without a word, he rips back the covers of the bed. He crosses the room when I don't move and tosses me in.

I expect him to join me, but he grabs the smaller woven blanket from the bottom corner and tugs it off the mattress, falling asleep in a chair by the door.

CHAPTER SIXTEEN
Kethi

Roxie is not sleeping. She started on the bed's far side, rolling with her back toward me, breathing purposefully in a regular cycle. When her purposeful breath did not work, she began groaning, flopping to her back, and staring at the ceiling of our room. She still could not sleep, so she groaned again, nestling with her face toward me. After another round of many breaths, she sighs and tries to lie on her stomach. She sighs and groans with frustration. She props up a leg, puts it back down, bends her knees, sits up against the wall, gathers the blanket between her knees, tosses it from her body, rolls it to the other side of the bed, and repeats the process. By the time her feet hit the room floor, the moon is at its peak in the sky.

She peeks at me in the darkness, and I pretend I am asleep. I am curious as to what she will do. Dragging the blanket from the bed, she wraps it around her body and carefully pads across the dirty floor. I can hear the fabric scrape against one of many items cluttering my floor and her hissing at the disruption. She pauses her advance, looking at me carefully before pressing forward again. When she is mere feet from my chair, she clears my ledgers from the seat beside it and curls up against the cushioned seat. A soft hum of comfort reaches my ears, and they perk at the sound.

I tilt my head further, watching her tug her knees up to her chest. She lays the blanket over her knees and rests her chin on them before whispering, "You can stop pretending you're asleep. I watched your eyes track me all the way over here."

"You should be in bed. It's much more comfortable." It feels dumb coming out of my mouth. Obviously, Roxie did not find comfort in our bed. Her lack of response only serves my point, and I continue, "Maybe you would be more comfortable at another Valkarran home?"

I thought all I wanted was her in our bed each night, warming my sheets with her intoxicating scent to convince her to spend time with me in the late and early hours. Yet, watching her struggle to sleep only made my hearts beat faster, and my breaths feel shallower as if I could feel her discomfort from across the room.

"No." She replies simply, yawning. "I would be equally uncomfortable. It's not about where I am; it's about what I see when I close my eyes."

"And what do you see?"

"I don't want to talk about it."

I'm torn between my desire to press the issue and my desire to see her happy. *Will talking about it help her sleep? Will she be more optimistic after a good night's rest? I always am, but I cannot make the same assumption about her. She is my ĝha – I can trust her to make good decisions for herself.*

"Should we speak of something else?"

"Like what?"

I sit up and grab the arm of her chair. Unlike in Wupeso, working and learning in a chair is common. We still sit on the floor for gatherings, or when we eat, it's important to the Baso Sheva to spend time close to the land, but in many Valkarran homes, we have chairs and tables for working and learning. Or, apparently, sleeping when you're angry with your *ĝha*. I drag her chair close enough to mine to feel her body's heat.

"How terrifying you can be?" I offer, though my tone is teasing.

Her eyes search mine, tracking across my face with concentration. Roxie is observant. I can distract her with enough pressure, but not for long. She seems to tear my teasing apart in her mind and settle on a conclusion I cannot see. As a result, she crawls from her chair into my lap, dragging her blanket with her.

"Exhausted is more like it. Keep away the nightmares, yeah?"

"What are *night-mares*?"

"Like a bad dream, but worse." She mumbles, though her voice is soft and quiet.

"Are you seeing these bad dreams now?" I ask, recalling her earlier words.

She shakes her head against me and mumbles, "New safe home."

"You feel safe?"

I do not get a reply, but her breaths soften, and the tension fades from her body. She does not stir when I gather her closer to my chest or wrap the smaller blanket around her. She does not let out a peep when I carry her to our bed. She burrows closer, keeping her hands tight against my chest. I watch her all night for a hint of movement, a clue to her bad dreams, but it never comes.

CHAPTER SEVENTEEN
Roxie

When my eyes open, they meet a wall of bright blue muscle, and I know the reason for the sudden disappearance of my nightmare plague. *The mate bond.* We didn't sleep together. We only *slept* together, which was enough for my broken brain to allow me some rest. If I had known about the sweet dreams, I would have dove straight into Kethi's waiting arms.

I learned to live with my new reality in the dozens of years since experiencing war trauma. The nightmares. I knew how disgusting humanity could be, the depths of hatred one person could feel for another, the thirst for blood eating at the hearts of certain souls. I learned what it meant to hate your job, to know what it felt like to have your trust broken by a child on the street.

Eventually, I went to space. Earth problems didn't exist there. There was never a war in the slick metal hallways lined with gold-leafed wallpaper and thick velvet carpets. I slept like a baby. The delineation between Earth and Open Space was a clear line drawn in red marker across my brain. The doors to my trauma were tightly closed and defended by the knowledge none of those people could reach me. Until the warning alarm started blaring while I was joking around with Jack and Ian. At that moment, it all came rushing back. My instincts went back on high alert, and the peace of space was ruined.

Every night I spent on Shojo was like old times. My nightmares mixed Earth trauma and Space trauma into one massive trauma soup. Sometimes, it would be some *V`òllø* child with a bomb strapped to their chest speaking gibberish, and instead of talking him down, I'd hug him until the second before the bomb went off, and I would be ripped from sleep. Other times, I'd be in space, and an enemy military, backed by chitinous spiders, would come to take us all prisoner. The aliens always watched on in glee as the humans were the ones to torture their own. The dreams were more like drug-fueled nightmares, where I was ripped under currents of blood created by my fallen teammates. I had missed sleep.

Last night I tossed and turned. The sheets were too scratchy, the bed was too empty, and my thoughts were too dark. *He'll kill you in your sleep*, my mind had whispered. I imagined it like the Kermit the Frog meme, hiding in the shadows with a dark hoodie covering his face, but I let the thought pass on by. Even though he infuriated me, I couldn't imagine hurting him permanently, and I doubted he could, either. So, I got closer to him.

I acknowledge that I'm glad he brought us to bed. He looked ridiculous, crumpled in the chair anyway. I would have been comfortable, but he is too big for even his furniture. This was much better.

"What is going on in your round little head, Sunshine?" He asks, though his voice is soft and low.

I take this as my opportunity to extricate myself from his arms. I push away from his chest, and the cool air of the bedroom slinks in, wrapping around me and leaving goosebumps along my skin. Without missing a beat, my mind reminds me that this sucks. It was nice to be held. *Gross.*

"Sunshine?"

"I slept through the night," I say by way of explanation. Like, can't he read my mind and understand? He needs to know how much that meant to me without me having to say it.

"Yes, good. No bad dreams?"

I think back to the night before. I didn't have any dreams at all. Nothing disrupted me from the pure blackness of rejuvenating sleep. Aside from some mumbling, I can't remember when we were back in the chair. My sleep was completely undisturbed. For the first time. In months. And aside from the small week sabbatical on the ship – in years.

"No bad dreams," I confirm. I stretch, wondering if I died on the ship and this is some kind of weird afterlife I'm trapped in. Luckily, the relief of a whole night's sleep rushes through me like a wave, and I stop second-guessing a good experience.

I'm the first to climb out of bed. From all the tossing and turning, I realized I still had my gun strapped to my leg, and when I slid it across the nightstand, it didn't help me get any more comfortable. Under the covers, I had stripped out of my uniform jumpsuit, which did nothing either. It seemed like I wasn't even comfortable in my own skin until I was pressed against Kethi.

Now, standing in only my underwear, the discomfort felt doubly true. I slip into my jumpsuit first, enjoying the buzz and slide of the zipper before putting my loaded holster back on. Once secure, I take the nine mil from the holster and count my bullets. Sixteen, as usual. Awesome.

I walk to the door and force my feet into my boots. I don't know when they got moved from beside the bed, but I wasn't about to ask any questions. I run a hand over my hair before realizing it's terrible and raking my fingers through it to smooth it out.

Glancing over my shoulder, Kethi is still in bed, staring at me. My heart feels like thunder in my chest, and I need to escape before the lightning feelings overtake me, and I can no longer make sense of my mind. If this is how I feel with his eyes on me, I don't want to risk anything more.

"I'm going to catch up with the girls. It looks like we're three slivers of the sun later than we agreed to anyway."

I expect him to fight back a little, to argue with me. I expect him to offer me breakfast or tell me I look pretty. Maybe he will tempt me to stay? But he doesn't. That wouldn't be true to Kethi's character. Last night he promised me he was playing the long game and the long game he would play.

CHAPTER EIGHTEEN
Roxie

"I can't believe this place. It's huge," Priscille says, spinning in her third circle to clock the multi-storied buildings. Murals of sand and mosaics of crystalline tile decorate most of the outer walls. It does feel a bit surreal.

"How were your host families?" I ask as we walk along the dusty road. They are easily wide enough for the flying mounts to land in, but we've yet to see another form of transportation as we walk along them.

The moment I closed Kethi's door behind me, the women were waiting, sitting in a circle, sharing some fruit and *okkoran* dust. I was so relieved I hugged Aston, and she ushered us away from Kethi's courtyard and deep into the city.

"Mine is amazing," Erja says, holding Ian's hand. Her younger brother is a quiet kid, and he doesn't do anything except walk alongside Erja and spin his colorful toy on his fingers. "Veo is an amazing host, and his son, Niri, gets along great with Ian. Right, bud?"

The little boy shrugs, spinning his toy and looking ahead. I can see Erja squeeze his hand before her smile softens.

"Ours is good too," Clara answers, "Once Priscille explained my sight, the mother told all the boys to help me learn some reliable paths through the house. They are a massive family, so their house is multiple stories, but the boys created a little barrier, so I know when I'm approaching the steps, and so Priscille doesn't have to be my personal walking stick."

Priscille scoffs, "Like Clara has ever needed me. Especially in their house. All the kids love her; they call her goddess and escort her wherever she might want to go."

Aston chuckles but remains surprisingly quiet.

"What about you, Aston?"

"Oh, yeah. My family is great. It's this poly woman with two *ĝhajo*, and they are all nice."

I can hardly believe this is the woman who faced her fear of the floating islands every morning to talk my ear off. Or the same Aston who paraded around Wupeso, arguing and peddling her thoughts about The Mate Debate.

"That's it? Really nice? Where's the Aston pizzaz?" Clara asks.

"What do you want me to say? The guys are both trying their damnedest to impregnate her. It's like an alien porno between the walls?"

"Uhm, yes," Clara exclaims, making the rest of the women giggle.

But Aston says, "Well, now you know."

"Someone is missing a certain alien fisher," Priscille teases, bumping her shoulder with Aston's. The redhead sighs, and the dam breaks.

"I thought he'd come after me. He's been irritatingly attached to me since we landed, and in Wupeso, it was like I couldn't do anything to lose him. I had to beg Kano to keep him busy long enough for me to get to take off. The moment we left Wupeso, and I couldn't see the island anymore, I felt like this deep disappointment I couldn't shake. As I hear aliens boning next door, I wonder, where's my freaking alien lover?"

"It sounds like you miss him," I tell her, trying to keep my amusement to myself.

"I don't miss him like that," She grumbles, "He's been the only constant since we crashed. Vera has Kano, you all have each other and your various hobbies, and I've got Llazho. Or I thought I did, but he's not freaking here."

"Did you really expect him to follow you across seas?"

"Yes," She says without fanfare.

"Good, because he did," I say, pointing toward the alien storming toward our group. You could tell he was a Wupeson from a mile away, but in case you couldn't...

Llazho approached like an angry wave. His sea-green skin was tight around tensed muscles, and his linen shirt was open and untucked. His face was a mask of barely contained rage and genuine admiration for the redhead beside me.

"Az-ton," He growls as he reaches the group. We expect him to say something more. We wonder if she will begin arguing with him, but instead, he grabs her by the waist and gently tosses her over his shoulder. To which she answers with an indignant gasp and begins pounding on his back.

"You let me down, you big oaf." She says, even as he tilts his head to the other women and begins walking away. On the island, Aston did say she thought soulmates would always find each other, but this can't be what she meant. Right?

"Should we stop him?" Priscille asks.

"Aston wouldn't appreciate it," I respond, watching Llazho swagger away. The other girls don't seem convinced. I'm not even convinced.

As we're about to go trailing after them to ensure everything is alright, Aston props herself up against his back and shoots us all a wink.

"She's going to be fine." Erja decides for the rest of us.

CHAPTER NINETEEN
Kethi

After a night in my bed with my ĝha nearby, I feel much more like myself. I hadn't realized how distracted I had been until I woke up this morning and hummed my way straight to the forge. Liro is already here this morning, dressed as my advisor and holding a few leaves of information. I don my apron and begin fanning the flames hotter.

"How did you convince her to stay with you?"

I glare at him, "How did you even hear that?"

"Are you joking? I'm your number one advisor; I station your spies, train your explorers, debrief your tradesmen. I know when you make a stupid decision."

"Xatsoe, then."

"Mom actually told me."

"Mom knows?"

"About that – "

"Brothers," Xatsoe begins as a puff of steam appears from the forge to announce her arrival.

I put the tool I had been working on previously into the forge and leave the metal to heat as I look between my siblings. As much as Xatsoe drove me mad, she was alive, a blessing from the Baso Sheva. *D'o go chu merchu.* However, her ability to dodge a plague did not release her from her responsibilities. Since so many of our women died, she is supposed to find her ĝha.

"You should be in Wupeso," I greet, sending another prayer to the Baso Sheva that this will be a quick visit before she departs. She tests my patience with each day she is not gone.

"I've decided not to go."

"You're one of the five women capable of being *ĝhajo* in Valkarra. You must go according to the terms of the agreement." Liro protests.

"I told you both not to barter with my life. It's not my fault you do not listen."

"And Mother told you he would do whatever he needed to win his *ĝha*," Liro reminds her.

My *jisa,* now working properly, soothes the tension that fights to take space between my horns. Siblings argue. It's a fact of life, but this was much larger than my sister's petty issues with a less-developed village.

"Kano and his men are expecting you," I explain, "Do you want to cause a war?"

"If the men of Wupeso want to fight over my presence, let them die for it." She huffs. I can see Liro tense beside her, and my own patience thins. He looks between my sister and me, wondering what I will say next.

I look at the forge and curse at the metal beginning to burn. Jerking it from the flame, I let it cool slightly before using my tools to reshape the pointed edge of the shovel. When I look back at my sister, she is standing with her horns tall and a hip cocked. I consider my following words carefully.

"What if I gave you a choice?" I ask, thinking about how upset my own *ĝha* was by me making decisions for her. Women are free creatures, which is not so difficult to understand.

"I have made a choice. One not to go. Why don't you honor that?"

"Because it's not a feasible choice," Liro growls, his anger sparking along his *jisa.*

"Liro is right. I have promised our five available women in exchange for those who journeyed here for a time. Your absence will not go over well with our allies in Wupeso."

With a huff, she asks, "What is this proposed choice?"

"If you choose to honor the deal we've made with Wupeso, which will put the other Valkarran women at ease and forge bonds with the human women in the other village, then I will allow you to begin traveling with Mother even though you do not have a *ĝha*. I will give you that freedom in exchange for the three sun cycles of necessary time I promised Wupeso."

"And if I choose not to go?"

"You will be under guard at all times and unallowed to leave Valkarra until you have a *ĝha* and a child. Not even to the peaks to visit with the Nusosan."

"So, if I go, I will gain more freedom; if I stay, I will become a prisoner. How is that a choice?"

"All choices have consequences," I shrug, returning to my work. The loud clang of my tools against the head of the flattening shovel echoes around us. When I am happy with the shaping, I leave the piece to cool and cross my arms over my chest. "So, what will it be?"

"I will go," She bares her fangs, "but I want you to understand this is not for you or Valkarra. This is for freedom."

"Of course," I answer, unsurprised.

We all stand still for a moment, sizing each other up. Three siblings with three different callings in this life, all important to Baso Sheva.

"Better get moving," Liro says, winking at Xatsoe and breaking the moment. She hisses in his direction before she gathers herself and leaves with her horns held high. Liro shakes his head in disbelief. Neither one of us has ever managed to make Xatsoe do anything she didn't want to do. Yet, somehow, she would be leaving for Wupeso today.

CHAPTER TWENTY
Roxie

The *tsare* in Valkarra is lighter with a more refined finish. That's what I think about when we find ourselves on a café patio, spread out on colorful threaded cushions, enjoying the afternoon sun. The establishment's owner pulled us in, promising delectable food and drink and great conversation. Supplying us with fresh *tsare* and a spicy dish called *echeno,* they had yet to disappoint.

I feel like a woman in a rom-com when my head tilts back to laugh at something, and like reality would do, I don't finish my laugh before a large shadow overtakes my space. Silence drops around the table, and I expect Kethi when I open my eyes. I could never be so lucky.

"Xatsoe," I say, imbuing as much cold as I can into my voice.

She is seething. Her violet eyes are blown wide and locked on me. I try a small smile, to which she answers with a snarl of fangs.

"Three sun cycles in Wupeso," She spits.

If I had any instincts left, my gun would be in my hand, but apparently, the warm Valkarran sun on a sandstone patio after a full night of rest has made me soft. So, instead of standing or telling her to back off or trying to avoid another disaster like the night before, I scoot my cushion to the side and offer her a seat.

For a moment, I think she will refuse. The woman is massive. Kethi is easily eight feet tall, maybe ten at the top of his horns, but Xatsoe is closer to eight at the top of her horns. This close, I can see her amethyst markings like veins along her arms and hands. She wears a dress like silk that wraps her lithe frame and leaves her toned sides entirely on display. Before I can rework my strategy, she sits.

We all watch in abject horror as she slugs back the remainder of the *tsare* from the bottle. Her tongue, shockingly dark, catches a drip of the sweet drink from her lip before she growls, "What do I need to know about the human women?"

"Excuse me?"

Literally the night before, Xatsoe left me high and dry in a city I had no bearings in, and now she suddenly cared about the human women?

"What do you *know* about human women?" She repeated as if I was slow and did not understand her question.

I look between Priscille, Clara, Erja, and Blossom and back. Xatsoe is waiting rather impatiently for an answer, but I have no idea what to tell her. I glance over at Ian, who is eating some kind of alien chicken nugget, much to Erja's delight. He seems oblivious to the entire interaction.

"Why do you ask?"

Her fists tighten and shake at her sides, but I watch her forcibly take in a breath. In a forced calm, she says, "Because I will be spending three days with the ones who remain in Wupeso."

"You're actually going?" I'm so full of disbelief; I couldn't mask it if I tried.

Her patience is at its end because she snaps at me. "Are you cursed? Of course, I'm going back. I am Princess of Valkarra, and I am *ĝha*-less. *I* must set an example for the people. *I* must act with them in mind. *I* must not truly live until I am attached via a bond dictated by the *great Baso Sheva*."

She catches her breath as I – we – process her words. Xatsoe is nothing like I expected a sister of Kethi to be. Her anger seems to seep across her *jisa,* rattling down her markings. Her displeasure with what she must do is evident, and I can't help but relate. I didn't ask to make first contact or ask for a soulmate, and I didn't ever expect that alien soulmate to have a sister.

Still, it's Clara who says, "The human women will not receive your anger well, so you should try to suppress it."

It takes her a few moments, but soon enough, she unclenches her fists, rolls her shoulders back, and murmurs, "Proceed."

With Blossom's help, we tell her all the information we've gathered about the humans in Wupeso. We explain the situation with Alba, her deceased husband, the baby she's caring for, and her daughter, Caroline. We tell her about Daria and her younger sister and Zach and the twins. I explain the deal with Aston and Llazho and how she should expect to be drafted into The Mate Debate, and I warn her against making her an enemy. Clara, who is closer to Cerridwen, explains, to the surprise of Priscille and Erja, that the women are already expecting their first half-human, half-*V`òllø* baby. Then, we get into the other details, and when we're content that she knows everything she may need to know, down to the rules of poker, Xatsoe offers her horns for a tangle.

I grip one with my hand, and she thanks me before standing from the table and leaving us staring after her in confusion. *Her and Aston in the same village is a riot waiting to happen.*

CHAPTER TWENTY-ONE
Kethi

The sun may be going down, but my time with Sunshine is just beginning. I was wrong if I thought it would be hard to find her. My people flocked to the human women, amassing into a crowd worthy of the Baso Sheva. Tereko and his *ĝha*, Kanji, are freely sharing their space. It seems like all of their needs have gathered around and traded for time around the women. Still, Roxie is like a ray of light. She stands out among the crowd for me.

As I approach, one of the other human women says something that makes the others laugh, but Roxie reaches for her tiny weapon. My people gather closer as she speaks. She calls it a *gun* and says it works better than an arrow.

I stop in my tracks and watch as she carefully draws it from the holster and sets it on the table before dislocating the parts in front of everyone. She keeps the front pointed away before she removes all the tiny metallic cylinders, placing them to her right. Next, she slides the top of the weapon off and twists a couple of cylindrical pieces out. Equally as fast, she slides them back into place, pops the top back on, and shoves the tiny metal cylinders back inside it, counting under her breath as she goes. The human women start clapping their hands, and the *V`òllø* tap their tails along the ground. Someone calls for her to do it again, but faster.

As if the first time was only practice, Roxie appeals to the masses. I watch her dexterous fingers fly across the weapon, and the metallic slide of the pieces coming apart clinks. From how my *ĝha* clung to such a weapon, I expected it to be more than a half-dozen metal bits. One of the smaller inner pieces falls to the table before her, and I hear her curse quietly. Swiping it back up with her next breath, she shoves everything back inside the *gun* and finishes securing the weapon together. Without the tiny metal droplets that go inside, I almost wonder if I could craft one of these myself. Roxie begins tucking away her *gun*.

That is when I arrive, interrupting the happy gathering. Some of my people tilt their horns in greeting, others salute with their tails, but most become quiet. As their King, I am generally liked, but I can be intimidating to those who don't know me. Thus, the silence.

This silence is not lost on Roxie as she shifts to look at me with my people. Her *gun* is tucked away once again, and her eyes circle around their sockets when she sees me. She looks to the sky, realizes night is approaching, and stands from the table.

"You don't have to go, do you?" The human named Priscille asks, her eyes darting between my *ĝha* and me.

"I promised Kethi I would spend the evenings with him," She explains to the others, "Thank you again, TK. Ladies."

She bends at the knees and tilts her upper body slightly, making the other women giggle. She bumps fists with the young human boy and approaches where I stand beside the porch steps.

I hold my hand out to her so she does not fall down the steps. I should have known better. She does another circle of her eyes and bypasses my hand instead of jumping over the small rail and falling a few feet to the ground. Panic sends my hearts beating, but Roxie lands on her own two feet without issue.

I clench my fists at my sides and force myself to take a small breath. When my eyes land on Roxie again, the corner of her lip is tilted up.

"Where to?"

CHAPTER TWENTY-TWO
Roxie

It's a wooden ship. There are docks and little rowboats tied off to them. It smells like the sea, plus something discernibly alien – like fish, but not. The water rocks beneath the dock, attracting my attention to whatever fears lurk beneath the depths. When my eyes trail far out enough that I have to shield my eyes from the sparkling water, there is a ship.

"We're going out there?" I ask, trying to keep the excitement in my tone to a minimum. Back on Earth, I chose the part of the military that stayed on land for a reason. However, that reason wasn't because I was scared of the ocean or the sky. I didn't want to be drowned or experience a controlled crash for fun. The running and obstacle courses were plenty.

"I want to show you something, and we would get there by ship, yes."

Excited energy courses through me, and for the first time since landing on this planet, I want to smile for real. So, when Kethi steps into a rowboat and offers me a hand, I take it. When he rows us out to the ship and his hands come to my hips, I ignore the fluttering nerves in my belly and focus on the warm tingle of his hands. I find my footing on the wooden ladder rungs. When we're standing on the deck of this surprisingly small ship, and he's rushing back and forth, preparing sails and heaving up the anchor, I let my smile go.

When his eyes find me again, he halts in place. He stares at me as if I'm some kind of carnival feature.

"What?"

"*D'o go chu merchu.*" *My energy is yours.* "You look beautiful."

I look down at my crumpled jumpsuit and shake my head in disbelief. Beautiful was always the word used to describe my sister. She was the pretty one, and I was... me. I never grew into my nose and always held a touch of extra fat in all the places my sister and mother were flat as a board. It didn't bother me unless some almond aunt commented or pinched my love handles. Since my dad came from a family of wasps, that was too often.

My sister was my greatest protector in those situations. She always cared about the things my parents didn't notice. If an aunt commented on my body, Satine was right there to tell them how my body was the least exciting thing about me and that they were doing me a disservice by talking about it rather than my many accomplishments. I always wondered if she needed someone to do the same for her, but by the time I realized she did, I already knew who I was, and I was out of the house, being that person.

Beauty didn't matter. Because my immediate circle didn't constantly stick me in a beauty box, I had the space to be intelligent, strong, and spirited. So, I leaned into those traits. Acing tests, joining the military, and speaking my mind became part of me. I kept my hair short because long hair felt vain – too much like I was trying to fit in. I focused on science and math and gained enough clearance in the military to be included in programs the public didn't know about. Over time, I became the bright, powerful version of me I assumed I was.

That's why, when Kethi repeats that I'm beautiful, telling me I'm so beautiful, he can't look away, a laugh bubbles from inside me until full belly laughs explode out, doubling me over. When his brows furrow, I only laugh harder. He looks so disheartened. I realize he's not joking.

When I stop laughing long enough to speak, I ask, "What else? Why do you like me?"

Kethi, ever the thinker, stops to consider his words. My smile is wide, and I feel better than I have since we landed – both physically and mentally. Under my feet, I feel the waves as they sway the boat. I can smell salt in the air and feel the breeze filling my lungs. It feels so human. So normal. Then, my *ĝha* speaks again, and I hear the translation through my earbud, and the normalcy dissipates.

"I love you because you are like sunshine, lighting everyone's darkest spaces and witnessing what they fear. I love you because, aside from your irreverence, you are warm and inviting. Though I value your irreverence, too, because it forces me to question my thoughts and test my curated patience. I love that you chose to stay with me through the nights because they are shorter than the days. And that you thought it would make a difference in my pursuit of you. Mostly, I love how, somehow, in a way I don't understand, you found your way through the stars and skies to Shojo, where I would see you for the first time, and you would touch me fearlessly and set my second heart beating so I might know true divinity."

By the time Kethi finishes, we are toe-to-toe again, and my heart is beating at double its average speed. He's still hunched over, but this time it's for me. If I reached up on my tip-toes, our lips would touch, and everything inside me burns to make that happen. Unbidden images from our moment in the forest flash through my mind, and heat pools in my belly. His breath is fresh and cool across my lips, and I can feel my muscles flexing, urging me closer.

Kethi smiles and steps back. The cold envelops me. It is so unexpected I whimper – which only makes his grin grow wider.

Frustration lances through me so fast that I whisper, "You were going to kiss me."

"Absolutely not," He says, heaving a rope upward at the back of the ship. He calls over the wind, saying, "That would break your boundaries."

CHAPTER TWENTY-THREE
Kethi

The sun is gone as the boat glides through the water, but I am unafraid. I've made this trip plenty of times with my mother, father, and siblings. Navigating the dark with only crystal lights, sails, and a rudder is nostalgic. Furthermore, I had a reason to do it tonight. Roxie will love it.

Where the water of the sea turns from clear, light blue to dark, churning waters the color of my mother's skin, and a bit further, there is an underwater cove. It is home to many beautiful creatures, but the principal being is the *korovò*. It's a massive, leathery beast with various reflective fins that catch the light of their bioluminescent texture and create a pattern of light, making it look like thousands of stars have scattered across the seas. And it is a sacred animal to the Baso Sheva.

As the ship approaches the cove, I turn my attention from my *ĝha* to the rudder, navigating us toward the edge of the underwater rock formations to avoid the rougher seas. It also allows me to have a better place to drop the anchor.

Meanwhile, Roxie leans against the railing on the bow, watching the waves lap against the wood. She has been quiet since our almost-kiss, speaking to me only to ask for directives or criticize my steering. When asked where she learned to navigate the seas on Earth, she openly admitted she'd never directed a ship in her life but guaranteed she could do a better job. When I offered her the chance, she told me that wasn't ideal gentlemanly behavior. I was only happy to hear her words.

"We are here," I announce, standing a body's length behind her. I hold one of the glowing crystal lanterns in my hand.

"I can barely see anything. What is it you wanted to show me?"

She is not looking at me. She has not even turned in my direction. It makes my hearts ache.

"Take my hand," I offer, holding it out to her. My fingertips brush hers, and she jerks them away roughly. "I did not mean to offend."

She turns toward me. Her eyes narrow, nearly cutting me off from their warm brown depths. Yet, they shine under the glowing stone lamp in my hands. I expect her to begin yelling at me, but instead, a liquid orb drops from her eye, skating down the rosy skin of her cheek. I don't know what this means, but it strikes fear in my heart, even as she brushes it away. I have no idea what to do, but another drop falls from her other eye, and she angrily grunts as she brushes it to the wayside.

"Show me what we are here to see," she demands, her voice cracking and rough.

The gentleman in me forces action, and I place her hand on my arm. Leading her to the ship's side, I close the openings on the crystal lamp and plunge us into complete darkness.

For a moment, we can see nothing. We hear the lap of the waves against the ship, smell the ozonic scent, and feel the prickle of anticipation leading to something special. Roxie's nails prick against my *jisa,* and I wonder if my fearless *ĝha* is not so fearless after all.

I scatter seeds from my pocket on the surface of the water. I've been carrying them since I finished at the smithy, waiting for this moment. Tiny *chyaŭ* glow as they move, heating the water and causing it to bubble around them.

Roxie gasps as their glow illuminates the water, revealing a semicircular rock formation that dips deep below the surface. Colorful plants ebb and flow with the currents from divots in the rock, and larger fish swim to capture the tiny *chyaŭ*. She mutters something under her breath when the bigger fish appear to eat the smaller creatures and become lunch instead.

All of this is part of the process of drawing out the beast I came to see, yet I find myself more fascinated by the changes in my *ĝha*'s face. Only moments ago, liquid she did not like was leaking from her eyes, and now her eyes are wide and clear, staring at the display of nature below.

As the *chyar ̈ú* begin to fill their bellies, their natural body heat cools, and the water's bubbling reduces to a small churn. Their glow dims, but their true predator has already found them. The plants along the wall begin to be dragged down by the displacement of water caused by the *koro̊vò*. Roxie gasps.

CHAPTER TWENTY-FOUR
Roxie

It's a whale. A massive, sparkly whale that makes the night sea look more like the night sky, but a whale nonetheless. Its mouth yawns wide, sucking in water and the tiny shrimp-creatures that made the water boil like a pot of tea. The ship rocks backward as the creature crests the surface, taking away the glow of the shrimps and replacing it with a resplendent light of its own. Its back is a vast expanse of glowing swirls and dots, reflecting blue, green, and silver in unrecognizable patterns. Like a whale on earth, it heaves a breath, blowing air out of a hole atop its head, misting the sky around us.

It speeds further from the boat, leaping into the air and blending with the stars on the horizon. Well, aside from its reflective tail, which shows the line where our boat meets the sea and Kethi's eyes watching me instead of the magnificence before us. The impending splash crashes, creating waves around us and spraying up against the railing.

As if one creature was not enough, it lets out a low rumble that resonates across the ocean's surface, and three more of these whales appear from the depths. They seem to speak to one another in ethereal words meant to sound like stars' given voices. A twinkling chime, a rhythmic beat, a radiant tone, and a low resonant rumble are carried across the water, harmonizing like a heavenly quartet.

The experience makes everything else fall away. The embarrassment I felt from Kethi's rejection seems like years ago. The fear I felt when the light diminished and I could not ensure our safety, was gone – crushed under the weight of these incredible beasts.

A sea of stars sparkles and reflects; they make a big pink dot of light, a sparkling shade of purple under the brush of the water. Tiny silver sparks flash as the four creatures glide and spin around one another, using their tails to create a storm of light and color.

It's almost like underwater fireworks, like stars racing by in the night sky. I want to catch a glimpse and make a wish.

I would wish for justice for women here, back on Earth. I hope the corporation I worked for is paying out the nose for the shreds of ship their finding now. And I hope the families who lost us to the skies get enough cash to retire them. Or maybe I would wish for a better mate, or *ĝha*, or whatever for Kethi. Someone who knows his customs and is happy to follow them. A *V`òllø* woman who loves to explore and prays to their special Baso Sheva. Or maybe I would wish I was different, that I was pretty and gentle rather than a strong and ruthless woman who has taken lives. Maybe I wish I could be the obvious debutant Kethi needs in his life. I'm not fit to be a city queen, even with the previous leadership under my belt. But I'm beginning to like him, and I wish that was enough for me to forget how stained and broken I am.

"They're incredible," I tell him, tearing my eyes from the sight.

Kethi's icy eye color narrows on me, bouncing around his sockets like I'm lines of a military chart being analyzed. His eyes are working so hard, I wonder how long they've been stuck to me, even though my heart knows the answer.

His voice is thick when he asks, "So you liked it?"

My smile is dimmer than before but still present. "I loved it. These creatures are unbelievable. Like some kind of astral whale."

He nods at my words, though I'm sure 'whale' translated more generally for him. It was exceedingly lovely of Blossom to outfit him with a translator upon his first visit to Wupeso. It was even kinder that she allowed him to keep it when he left.

"They speak to one another through all those tones and notes. Like *ĝhajo* when they become bound, if you touch the water's surface, you develop a new understanding of their sounds. Their language."

I'm sure he didn't mean it as an invitation to jump in the alien sea, alone, in the dark, but I took it that way. His eyes widened slightly as I slid the zipper of my jumpsuit down my body, letting the stiff fabric crumple at my feet. Toeing off my boots, I can see him trying to come up with an argument. His color widens further when I drop my earbud in my boot. He knows it's probably not safe. He knows he doesn't want me to get hurt. Hell – the boat is an entire story above the sea line. Yet, he doesn't stop me when I walk to the edge, climb the small banister, and dive face-first into the water.

CHAPTER TWENTY-FIVE
Kethi

For a moment, I wonder if my *ĝha* will jump off every precipice I put her on. Her lithe body was graceful, tumbling toward the water with pointed hands and held breath. The water splashed around her, and I hoped for her sake it didn't attract an angrier beast. Worse, she didn't surface. I did not see her emerge for one, two, three breaths.

Leaning over the rail, I seek her form in the dark waters. I am moments from jumping in after her, clothing and all, when she reaches the surface with a sputter.

"*Fuck*, it's cold," she says, brushing wet strands from her face and blowing away droplets of water. Her eyes squint closed momentarily as her legs kick beneath the water. Then, she's smiling up at me from nearly three of my heights below. "Are you coming in?"

Was I going to jump in as she did? It had been a long time since I gave myself to the wisdom of the *korovò*. Yet, they always had something to say to me. I watched them in the distance, seeing my *ĝha* swim in their sea of stars. The light glinted across the surface, blurring under the churn of her legs and arms.

"I believe one of us should stay dry," I call down, even as I feel the press of the Baso Sheva.

Her brows furrow as she remembers she left her earbud tucked inside her shoe.

"The earbud situation is a bit annoying, don't you agree? Maybe we should get married like Vera and Kano." Her words sound sincere, but I cannot tell with the humans. So, I tilt my horns in agreement, and she nods. "Would you be a good husband, Kethi?"

I am eager to be her partner in this world, so I tilt my horns with enthusiasm, shouting down the human word, "*Yes.*" It feels odd on my tongue, but I'm pleased with myself when she realizes I've understood her and we've communicated.

Her smile, which she has given me so freely this evening, turns wicked. "A good husband joins his future wife for a midnight swim. I mean, if there are whales, there could be sharks."

In the earbud, '*shark*' does not translate well. Instead, the earbud defines it as a many-toothed, aggressive sea creature. Unfortunately, we have many of those here on Shojo, and the reminder is enough to lure me into the water. Dumping my clothes carefully in a pile beside hers, I take the rungs down to the water's surface.

It isn't particularly cold, but it's not warm either. With the protection of my *jisa,* I'm not as sensitive to the changes in temperature as Roxie seems to be. However, I feel warm under her gaze as my body enters the water.

It's been a long while since I've swam in the sea. In fact, my father was still alive at the time. It was him, Liro, and I – a male's trip since my mother brought Xatsoe on her first voyage. Xatsoe was proud of the map she brought back, and Liro was proud of the empty shells he free-dived for. It has been many seasons since.

I let the water lap over my shoulders before dunking my head under the water and pushing toward my *ĝha.* Surfacing before her, I can feel her little legs displacing the water around us. Her eyes meet mine, and I admire their warm color. Then, the whales begin to sing. She turns to face their tune.

CHAPTER TWENTY-SIX
Roxie

He will be your peace of mind. They seem to whisper directly to my mind. I don't have to ask to know they're talking about the *V`òllø* man in the water with me, that's swishing his arms to keep him above the surface. I don't ask them for more or confirmation as they press further into my mind, showing me exactly what they mean.

Swirling clouds sit among the beautiful alien trees in the mountains of Valkarra, and he is three steps behind me. I can hear his soft breaths as we hike up the mountain. I'm panting like a dog. We're searching for something special, but I don't know what it is. Then, the sunlight breaks through the trees and hits my face. I stop and take a breath. The fresh smell of dirt and fragrant flora invades my lungs, baked into the air by the sun's warmth. Next thing I know, he's holding me in his arms.

The scene changes, and we're standing on the docks where we came from. Kethi's hands work down my arms, and my tiny hands rest in his huge ones. His eyes are like pin-tops on me, and I am still breathless. He's whispering to me, but I can't hear exactly what he's saying, only feeling the comfort it brings me. He spins me, and we dance in his bedroom. I'm laughing, and my hair is long. It flings out and slaps his chest. That's when I notice, my gun is across the room, my belly swells, and his same shimmering *jisa* covers my skin.

I'm dropped back into the present moment, and the stars of the astral whales disappear beneath the surface. They plunged Kethi and me into darkness. The cool water laps against me, but before I can panic, Kethi grabs my arm and leads me to the boat. When I feel the rungs under my fingers, I climb with him, two steps behind.

We're both silent under the crystal lights on the boat. Kethi doesn't say anything as we get dry, but his shoulders are tense when he lugs up the anchor. I don't know what the whales did to him, but we returned to Valkarra without a word.

CHAPTER TWENTY-SEVEN
Roxie

Pounding on the door wakes me from my dreams before the women let themselves into Kethi's bedroom. Kethi is already gone, but I'm not surprised. It must be close to noon by now. By the time we got back to Valkarra and through the village last night, we were both so tired we collapsed into bed together in silence. And I had another night of uninterrupted sleep. My only dreams were remixes of whales in starry skies and dancing with Kethi on the water's surface. Romantic shit.

"Good morning," I grumbled, sitting up in bed. I'm half-naked because I left my gun and jumpsuit, and boots in a pile on the floor last night.

Priscille, Clara, and Erja enter together, utterly uninterested in my indecency. They make themselves at home. Priscille sits in one of the wooden chairs with her knees tucked into her chest, tapping the other for Clara. Meanwhile, Erja finds a spot on the edge of the bed.

"Tell us everything," Clara demands, her excited smile brightening her face.

"About?" I ask, throwing the sheets away from my body and stepping into my filthy jumpsuit before deciding against it. Stripping it away, I begin rifling through the stack of clothes Kethi had brought me (even though I had my clothes from Wupeso).

"Oh, please," Priscille groans. "Don't play dumb. You're too smart for that."

A smile tilts my lips, and Erja gasps. Immediately, my hands go searching for my gun before she starts laughing.

"What?"

"I haven't seen you smile in a while."

"I smile all the time."

"No, you don't," Priscille cuts in.

"You don't," Erja confirms.

"Tell us about your date," Clara demands, reiterating her snoopiness from earlier.

"It wasn't a date," I explain, choosing a silky wrap top and some well-tailored linen pants. With them on, I feel a little like I work at a bank, but my thigh holster looks good against the linen and is comfortable. Deciding to throw them a bone, I say, "He did agree to marry me, though."

Priscille snorts, "He agreed to marry you the moment his second heart started beating for you."

Her voice is like a mimic of Kethi, making my chest ache for some reason. "He knows what he wants and is a little flowery about it. So what?"

"All of them are a little flowery," Clara says, "All the guys in the family I'm staying with are so flirty. They call me 'goddess' and offer me anything I could need."

"Yeah, it was cute at first, but now it's getting annoying," Priscille adds.

"We're losing the point here. Roxie and Kethi are getting married. Are you excited?" Erja redirects.

I shrug. Excitement might be a stretch, but I knew the whales were right - Kethi brought me peace. It was noticeable in how he kept my nightmares away and how I barely thought to touch my gun around him. The earlier sickness made it obvious there was no easy way out, and would it really be so bad to have such a beautiful, simple man looking out for me? No. It wouldn't be bad at all.

"I'm just ready to have what Kano and Vera have," I admit to the women.

"Oh! Yay." Clara exclaims, clapping her hands. "Doesn't this mean we get to have a big festival? A celebration?"

"It did in Wupeso." Priscille agrees. "Valkarra seems different."

"How different can it really be?"

The answer: As contrastive as apples and oranges. In Wupeso, it was straightforward. Kano announced their impending wedding at dinner, and the festival began the next day. No one pressured the human women to join, but we were all still welcome, and then the *r¨uṣad'ù* happened. Vera added a human touch, yet suddenly she arrived at the *peholoe* loft with a pet drake the next day. We don't know what happened in the cave, but Vera assured us we would all survive our own if it ever came to that.

I'm not so sure she had the knowledge to say such as we walk together through the streets. The *V`òllø* are all whispering. They exchange meaningful glances as we pass, keeping their horns down as if they're not feet taller than us — as if we can't clearly see their faces. They have gossip. They all *know*.

It's confirmed moments later by a beautiful woman standing in the street. That is when I know it's really real. I'll be bound to my alien soulmate within days. And I'm okay. The world isn't ending because I found someone who makes me happy.

"Roxie Holt!" The *V`òllø* woman exclaims, joining the bubble of human women. My hand instinctively reaches for my gun, but I force it to my hip as she reaches for me. At the last possible second, she presses her long blue hands to her legs instead and gives me a fanged smile.

"I'm Serkha. Kethi's mother."

The world seems to zoom in on this one moment. I plant my feet to keep from swaying as I inspect the woman with more care. Serkha is his mother. This beautiful, sapphire-skinned *V`òllø* woman with kind eyes and eclectic clothes is his mother. His mother stares at me like I'm the lost arc and obviously knows me, while I know nothing of her. His mother, who tilts her head at my tight smile.

"Did Kethi not tell you I would seek you out today?"

Clara speaks for me since I'm frozen like a glacier, icy and stone-cold.

"He didn't have the chance. Roxie has been catching up on some much-needed sleep." Blossom translates.

Serkha smiles at the other women as if delighted that they are with me, paying particular attention to Blossom. She is magnanimous toward us, especially me, as she invites us to her home for tea – or words that translate as tea. Which Priscille eagerly accepts in the same breath as my refusal.

Serkha's horns jerk to the left, and she reels back. As if gathering her wits, her eyes narrow and widen rapidly before settling at midsized. I see exactly where Kethi gets it when she schools her face and says, "I insist. It is tradition, after all, to stay with your new family members leading up to the *r¨uṣad'ù.*"

My own surprise must be evident because Serkha's beautiful eyes narrow. "He didn't tell you anything, did he?"

CHAPTER TWENTY-EIGHT
Kethi

"There is no way you have already won the affections of your *ĝha*," Liro grumbles as I saunter into the forge the following sun cycle. He is wrong, of course. As my brother, he can see it in how I walk, the strong pulse of my *jisa* on my skin, the glow in my markings.

"She asked me to bond last night."

"Sheva bless me, I do not need those details."

"Not like that, you *niliofe*. Roxie wants to go through with the *r̈ůṣad'ù*."

"It's good you already arranged for the hunt next sun cycle, it seems," He explains, making notes on his records.

Liro was my advisor long before I was Rogeshu. In our youth, he always told me how to act and what was proper. He explained our parents' rules in a way that made more sense. He would break them and tell me it was because he was younger. Many of the rules no longer applied to him – at least until Xatsoe came, then they applied to Liro but not her.

Thoughts of the night before rip at my attention. Roxie looked beautiful – standing at the bow, falling gracefully into the water, emerging on a surface of starlight. My hearts beat like wings at the memory of her words. *Maybe we should get married like Kano and Vera. Would you be a good husband, Kethi?*

The forge's heat presses against me, soothing my nerves and focusing my mind. Liro is smirking at me, the color of his eyes narrowed like tree needles. I ignore him, hammering away at my next project.

Since Roxie has been in Valkarra, my tool production has improved. I've managed to repair my entire backlog and create new stock for the storefront, all before the sun's peak each day. Thanks to Liro's constant rambling about what it means to be Rogeshu, my evenings were also filled. While daydreaming about Roxie, Liro would stand at my side and walk me through the needs of our people. Walkway maintenance, goods to be negotiated from the Nusosan people or the Wupesons, village complaints between *V`òllø* men who desire to measure horns. Then, we'd organize my schedule, and I'd finally be released to see my *ĝha*.

"Kethi," Liro calls, dragging my attention back to him. "Will she be staying with our mother?"

"Of course, I told Mother at the first sliver of the sun," I respond, cooling the tool in my hands.

"And did you tell Roxie?"

The tool clatters to the stone floor sparks flying up around my feet. I am the worst of husbands, and the *r¨uṣad'ù* has not even happened yet.

CHAPTER TWENTY-NINE
Roxie

My alien soulmate grew up here. At least, based on what I know from Wupeso, that's how it works. *V`òllø* families stick together until they have families of their own. Then, when you become older and lose your *ĝha*, you live among the other *peholoe* and share your wisdom with all those young families. This means until Kethi became the Valkarran leader, he lived here.

The homes in Valkarra are much more earthlike. In a square foyer, we remove our shoes and tuck them against the wall. Slipping through a sliding door, the roof gains height, opening up high above me while all the furniture is close to the floor where children can reach it.

Structurally, it looks almost like the *peholoe* loft, but not quite. A blue crystal box sits inside an alcove on the wall like the ice chest they keep on the loft floor. A massive slice of tree stump acts as a table nearby. To the left, woven mats sat in the center of three walls stuffed with relics, scrolls, and books.

Books. Real books with wooden bindings line the shelves beside fancy shells, unusual rock formations, and crystals in colors I haven't seen before, like green, purple, and black. I take a book the size of a cracker box from the shelf and open the cover. It's stuffed full of maps. Beautiful maps inked onto those fibrous leaves Aston made Vera's wedding cards out of. I rub my finger against the solid blueish-black line. Ink.

I place the book back on the shelf and pull out another. This one has many lines of characters that start at the center of the page and circle outwards from there, all the way into the margins of the page. I inspect another. This one holds sketches of different flora and fauna, with what I can only imagine are descriptions in scripted circles beneath it. I slide the book back onto the shelf.

When I look over at the others, Priscille is losing her mind. Like a crackhead getting its first hit in months, she opens one of the books with the dried pages and sniffs it like a line of cocaine. Her following smile is disturbing at best, horrific at worst. Though, Blossom is intrigued.

The synthetic intelligence is gentle and purposeful as she flips through each page of the books scanning and chirping away her findings.

"There are other discovered lands my tools did not reach. There are other sentient beings." I could swear I heard the awe in her robotic voice.

"This is cool," Erja says, showing Ian the colorful wooden toys in the corner. "They are like your blocks at home, Ian." He builds with them almost immediately.

The room's back wall is made of a glass-like crystal that looks out over the riverside farms and allows the sunlight to stream through. Even with the light, they placed dozens of glowing crystals throughout the space.

On the opposite side is the entry and three more doors that open and close like the ones on Earth. While the other women peruse the shelves and Blossom spills facts to Clara, I open the door beside the entry.

The bed stretches along the back wall, and two tables in front of it on either side. Clutter litters the space. A pack of fabrics bursting from it sits to the side, a basket full of feathers and jars is on one of the tables, and a stack of books sits next to a gelatinous-looking object with a needle attached.

"This is where I sleep," Serkha says, standing beside me. By the time she spoke, my hand was already unlatching my gun, but I slid it back into my holster as I looked up into her eyes. *She doesn't know you. This isn't Earth. This isn't the S.S. Herculean. You don't need your sixteen bullets.*

She looks inside her room, and I wonder if she's trying to imagine it through my eyes. With a shrug, she steps away, and I close the door.

"You will be in the final door down the hall. It used to be Kethi's. Xatsoe sleeps in the center. She will return for your *r̈ ůṣad'ù*, but I would not bother her. She is like the beasts of the woods when disturbed."

I take the opportunity to open the door to my room, and the setup is similar to Serkha's, but it is clean. A simple fur rug is laid across the center of the floor, and one table sits beside the bed on the left side of the room. Fresh blankets folded in neat triangles are arranged like a square on the bed. The wall is made of slats similar to the ones in the *peholoe* loft, and I press many open to allow in a breeze.

"Thank you," I say, looking back at Serkha.

She studies me. The color of her eyes shifts smaller and more prominent as she takes in my features, catalogs my height, and notices my hand unconsciously tapping my weapon holster. I wonder what she will say about me. I can practically hear my own mother's nitpicking. *Honey, stand up straighter. Honey, your hair is too long. Honey, I love you, but you are too much. Men don't like that. Honey. Honey. Honey.* But Serkha says none of that.

Instead, she hits me with, "I can see why he calls you Sunshine. You are a dazzling spot in this dimming world."

As if she hadn't just blindsided me with kindness, she turned to the other women, "Shall I prepare some food and tea?"

I am stuck in my place as the other human women flock to my new alien mother-in-law.

CHAPTER THIRTY
Kethi

Baso Sheva, she's beautiful. Dressed in traditional Valkarran custom, Roxie is resplendent, like the first sliver of sunlight. She stands tall and formidable, like the mountains framing Valkarra. She is as harmonic as my favorite song. Roxie is an extra chord that belongs to me, my family, my life, like I belong to hers.

Liro's horn knocks against my own, "Are you going to stare, or shall we join our mother for family dinner?"

I rub my horn where he knocked it, though that hasn't hurt since they were soft as children. He huffs in disbelief before pushing the crystalline door to our mother's living area open.

Without the door obscuring her, I'm struck immovable again. Roxie laughs at something my mother says, a cup of *tsare* held in her hand. Her loose hair falls around her shoulders like a pot of black ink. It leaves her neck and collarbones bare. My fangs ache to scrape against her skin. When my mother whispers of my arrival, her eyes trail across the floor to meet mine. They steal the breath from my lungs. My twin hearts cease beating. Then, she smiles in my direction, and the world again rights itself.

How did I ever believe I would live without her?

"Are you going to just stand there or join us for dinner?" My mother calls, stealing my attention from Roxie. Roxie smirks at my distraction, putting her head down as I step into the room.

My mother has prepared an incredible spread for the evening, and yet, my only concern is for the enjoyment of my *ĝha*. She is still sitting here, so I assume she is not angry at me for my miscommunications. I take a seat beside her.

"You cannot sit next to your *ĝha*," My mother spouts immediately, dragging me up by the arm and across the short table from her. Roxie closes one eye in my direction, and I worry my lip with a fang. *What does it mean?*

Liro sits beside my *ĝha,* and my hands become fists at my side. He smiles down at her, fangs and all.

"I'm Liro, Kethi's brother. I'm sorry you were sick. I told my brother it was stupid to leave you in Wupeso when he knew you were his *ĝha.*"

"And with charm like that, he didn't listen?" She asks, smirking in Liro's direction. I hate that he can earn even a slight tilt of her lips when I had to work so hard for my smiles. My jealousy knows no bounds.

"You were adamant about staying with the human women," I persist. Her exact words included how she would *never* come to Valkarra, but I do not speak back those words. I would be happier for it if I never had to hear them again, even from my own mind. Roxie's smile falls slightly, dimming her light.

"It had been a rough night," she explains, reaching for her tiny weapon. Her fingers fumble at the clip holding it in place before she fists her petite hands. She spreads them across the table's surface and forces herself to smile. I can tell because it does not reach her eyes. I want all her smiles to reach her eyes.

Before I can begin running through dozens of ridiculous ideas for cheering up my *ĝha,* my mother intervenes. The scent of fire-roasted roots and *okkoran* spiced fish wafts between us, drawing our attention. Liro is the first to dig in, flaking off a slice of the fish and tearing some crispy skin with it. My mother, acting much more like the host than she ever did in my childhood, serves Roxie a plate and finds her seat at the head of the table.

"It is not the most decadent of foods, but it is Valkarran tradition for the *velahipu.* You must eat it all. Or I will be offended."

Roxie's eye circles roll in their sockets, but she takes a bite and hums her delight. My eyes are trapped on her mouth. Her tiny pink tongue grazes her bottom lip as she nods at my mother. *I wonder how it tastes.* In the woods, she was incredible. It was a miracle we ever stopped.

"Kethi," my mother interrupts my thoughts, cooling my face to the color of ice. "You must eat to content as well. It's tradition."

"Yes, *ngi.*"

The eating portion of the night goes without any more bumps. Liro keeps his mouth shut, mostly because he stuffs it with every unwanted bit of food as if competing with the city's compost pile. He even licks flesh from the bones of the fish, hissing when one of the fragile pointy bits stabs him in the lip.

My mother does most of the talking, engaging Roxie in conversations about what to expect for the rest of the moon cycle and eventually our *r̈ u̧sad'ù.* When Roxie questions her about caves and beasts, my mother is sensitive to our allies in Wupeso when explaining the differences. Her personal opinion is that the olden way of the *r̈ u̧sad'ù* is barbaric, and the Baso Sheva would tell us if our more modern equivalents were wrong. My father, when he was still alive, still made them participate in both. She mentions the hunt.

Through a mouth full of masticated food, Liro notifies my mother and my *ĝha*, "The hunt starts tomorrow."

"Tomorrow? So soon?" My mother asks.

"Yes, Kethi planned ahead."

I look at my *ĝha*, expecting distrust, more anger. I wonder how she will punish me when she says, "Great. I'd love to go."

Sheva curse me.

CHAPTER THIRTY-ONE
Roxie

Serkha's home is still dark when I leave my room to join the hunt. So, I wasn't expecting to see her or Priscille. Especially not together, huddled over a book beside a glowing crystal speaking in hushed tones.

"Do you think that's why I'm here? To strengthen my faith?" Priscille whispers the best she can – which is to say, not at all. Priscille is one of those women who is meant to be heard. Her voice carries more weight than most. She's meant to be heard because she doesn't use her words to lie or deceive.

"The Baso Sheva works in peculiar ways. Maybe it is worth considering They know your God. That deities work together for the greatest good of their children."

Priscille nods, her head bowed toward the book in her arms. Without wanting to interrupt, I shut the door loud enough to announce my presence. Serkha looks up first, a smile gracing her sharp face. Priscille follows suit, rolling back her shoulders and shutting the book.

"Will you ladies be joining the hunt today?" I ask, stretching my neck to both sides. Kethi glared in my direction when I announced I would be joining, and Liro told me all about the hiking as if it would deter me.

But truthfully, nothing sounded more amazing than hiking alone, being with my thoughts, and finding a use for my gun. Finding a use for sixteen static bullets. I check for the fifth time it's strapped to my waist and smile when I feel the cool metal beneath my palm.

"Not me," Serkha says, "I must prepare my ship to leave after your *r̈ușad'ù*. We will be going on our longest expedition yet." She gives a pointed look to Priscille, who smiles in her direction.

"I'll come to the opening ceremony. All the boys in the house we are staying in are going, and Clara will be waiting for me."

"You don't want to hike with me?" I ask, already knowing the answer. I'm only offering out of kindness.

"Can I be honest with you, Rox?" Priscille asks, hanging onto my elbow. I truck her out the door as Serkha walks behind us.

"Of course. Always."

"There is nothing I want to do less than chub-a-rub-rub my thunder thighs together for hours seeking some deity-blessed beast. I know this fit makes me look like hot stuff, skinny mini and all that," she runs her free hand over her curves, "but my thighs have touched since I was thirteen, and in this heat, it's chafe-city. If God wanted me to be a hiker and hunter, he would have made me lean like a mountain cat. But thus, he made me with child-bearing hips, and I wouldn't have it any other way."

I look over at Priscille with a raised brow. She raises one right back. Then, she smiles, and it makes me smile, and we bend together, our heads giggling like schoolgirls, paying zero attention to where we're heading.

Priscille gets oddly severe momentarily, resting her forehead against mine as she says, "You seem happier, Rox."

Do I? I think about how easily I'm smiling and laughing with her, and she might be right. But instead of admitting such, I laugh it off and roll my eyes. Grabbing her hand, I drag her along. At least until we run right into the back of Clara.

Our friend bumps the man before her, breaking Priscille and me apart at the arms. One dark, human-looking hand steadies Clara. Like a scene in a movie, Priscille and I tilt our heads back to look at the face of the man growling at us and gasping in unison.

Wings, covered in opalescent white feathers, jut widely from the man's back. His deep umber skin is smooth and trailed through with violet tattoos. He narrows his brows, baring his teeth in what is sure to be a snarl, but Clara interrupts him.

"Sol, wait. It's my friends."

Anger immediately flees his features as his attention is returned to Clara. He loosens the hands on her waist and arm before stepping back.

"Commander Roxie Holt," I offer my hand, acting braver than I feel. The *V`òllø* are intimidating but gentle giants. I know nothing of this man, this alien, other than that his name is Sol, and Clara knows him.

"King Solispera of the Nusosan people of the mountains. I ally us with Kethi Rogeshu and his people," the king with wings replies as he takes my hand. When I keep a firm grip and shake it up and down, his eyes widen slightly.

"It's a custom from my planet. Our planet. Earth." I explain, releasing his hand and twining my fingers with Priscille's.

"I'm Priscille," She says, keeping her hands to herself. *Smart.*

"These are your friends, Clara-*weya*?"

"Yes, and Erja and Ian and Blossom."

"Very well, I will leave you in their care, *liye*. Will you be at the feast? After the hunt?"

"I can be."

"Please do." He replies, dragging his hands from her body. "I will speak with you thence."

"Okay," She squeaks.

We all wait in silence until he is out of sight and we can no longer hear him. When we are confident he is gone, Clara whispers, "Is he hot? He sounds hot. I want to feel him."

"He's worth the heat of hell." Priscille whispers, "The man looks like sex."

"Roxie, is it true? Pris says they are all hot."

"They are all hot, but that man is," I pause, words leaving me as another man appears. One I'm much more familiar with.

Dressed in nothing but a pair of loose square trousers and a leather quiver, Kethi smiles and taps horns with the other *V`òllø* men. His mate marks are on full display with the rest of his markings, and suddenly all I want is to trail those lines with my tongue. Like vines, they crawl over his sides, disappearing beneath his waistband. My head tilts as I wonder exactly what he's hiding beneath there.

"He's what?" Clara asks, snapping me out of my dirty dreams.

My tongue feels thick as I mumble, "Very attractive."

She groans, throwing her hands up in the air. "The hottest voice in all of Shojo, and I can't even get details."

"All I could see was how angry he was because we bumped you. The protective hands he had on you. The guy wouldn't mind you feeling all over him." I mutter, tracing my eyes over my own *ĝha's* body.

Clara grabs our still-joined hands, "Pris, we have to go to the celebration tonight. I have to get close to him again."

"Okay, okay! We'll go. Relax."

Clara jumps up and down, finding her way up Priscille's arms before flinging her arms around her neck. "Thank you!

Thank you, thank you, thank you. You won't regret this. It will be great. I promise."

Though Priscille smiles, she says, "The regret is already sinking in."

CHAPTER THIRTY-TWO
Kethi

Going into the woods with my *ĝha* alone is the stupidest idea I've ever had. Last time we were in the woods alone, my tongue was between her – *stupid, stupid, stupid.* Worse, I could feel her eyes on me earlier. I was talking to the men, and the markings across my body warmed, but the first sliver of the sun had not even arrived. When I found her in the crowd, she was already speaking with the other human women, and I've been wondering how to get her eyes back on me since. Maybe *ĝhajo* are the Baso Sheva's way of keeping *V`òllø* weak.

"You coming?" Roxie asks, looking down the trail at me.

The sun is beating down on us now, my *jisa* strengthens to keep me cool against its heat, but Roxie's skin glistens with liquid that shines under the sunlight. We're surrounded by trees, moss, and fresh air, yet the warmth of the passing slivers reaches us.

"I'm right behind you, Sunshine." I pant, watching her legs flex against the material of her trousers. I will have a hard time finding anything out here with her around. All I want to do is tackle her to the dirt and feel her writhe underneath me. Does your *ĝha* count, Baso Sheva?

"Don't you ever hike around? These mountains are beautiful."

My heavy breathing is making me feel inept. "I don't oft have the time."

She hums, unimpressed with me and dragging us further into the mountains.

"What's your favorite color?" Roxie asks, resting her hands on her knees as we take a break.

I want to tell her I have many favorite colors. The warm brown of her eyes, the slick black of her hair, the rosy tone her cheeks have now. I want to tell her it's the lush, vibrant green of these mountains or the warm tawny glow of the sand, or maybe the clear blue of the river cutting its way through the land beneath us, but I settle for the answer I've had since I was a child.

"Black, like the nettle flowers."

"Black is my favorite, too."

My heart warms, and she shifts on her rock, moving closer to me. I don't know if she realizes that she gravitates closer to me, places a hand on my skin, or smiles when she hears my voice. I don't point it out.

"Is it everything you thought it would be?"

"What?"

"The hunt, your wedding festival? Me?"

My first thought is to tell her no. I didn't plan for my *ĝha* to join me on the hunt. I didn't expect the evening slivers to wane with no kill in sight. My wedding festival may have never happened if it were not for her. But, it is times like these that I am grateful my mother taught me to think before I speak because those words would have hurt my *ĝha*.

"This is more than I could have desired."

"Hm," She hums once again, unimpressed.

The darkness has overtaken the sky by the time either of us sees something worth killing. Roxie has her gun out, pointed at the *gego* long before I can respond with my bow. In the darkness, she takes aim, and I know she will miss before she does. I let out a careful breath, and her finger curled around the tiny metal piece. She plucks it to the point of tension before a loud crash sounds from the woods, spooking the beast.

Her shoulders drop, her free hand becomes a fist, and she shoves her gun back in its pocket so hard the skin of her arm shakes.

"Fuck!" Her voice is so loud it ruffles the smaller wildlife. We are deep within the woods now, and with the sun gone from the sky, we will only see more creatures – some kind, some volatile. The ones attracted to the noises are the ones we should be fearful of, though I don't tell her such.

"We will find another beast," I assure her, wondering if I should offer to let us rest. Roxie hasn't eaten since our last break, and I wonder if she would like one of my pouch snacks.

"Or maybe we won't. Maybe this *r̈ușad'ù*, this wedding isn't as meant to be as we believe. Maybe the bond works differently with humans."

I tread carefully, "How so?"

"Maybe it's not as strong. Maybe it's not this once-in-a-lifetime phenomenon, but you have multiple, and if I go away, someone better will come along."

"No. That is not – "

"How do you know?" She pauses, and when I do not answer, she says, "That's right! You can't. Because there have never been human women here. I'm probably not even your *ĝha*. I'm probably stealing it from someone who actually deserves you. Thousands of lightyears from Earth, and I still can't – "

"Stop!" Anger is boiling inside me like burnt metal in a crucible. "The *ĝhajo* markings do not matter because I *love* you. You fill my mind every sliver of every day. I cannot work without knowing what you are doing. I cannot sleep when you are not in my bed when your scent is not in my room. Half the time, I cannot even breathe when you are not near me. I forget as if nothing else matters but knowing where you are and ensuring it is near *me*."

My whole body feels as though it is buzzing. It feels like her distinct essence is burning through me, like sunlight itself is purifying me for good. For *her*. I am barely restrained, calling on all of my willpower to not prove it to her with my words, mind, and body. I want to prove it to her. I want to give her everything.

So when she looks at me and her nose wrinkles and that soft, humming "hm," leaves her mouth – the tether in me snaps. Roxie is mine, and she will *know* it.

CHAPTER THIRTY-THREE
Roxie

I've messed up. BIG.

One moment, our chests are heaving, there is a foot between us, and neither of us can stand to be in the same clearing. The next, Kethi's arm wraps around me like a vice, lifting me from the ground and trapping me against his chest. His eyes are wide and so dark they look nearly black in the darkness. His breaths are rough, and I feel each cascading across my lips, down my chest. It feels erotic, stimulating parts of me I forgot about.

Then, I realized I hung limply from one of his arms and immediately began to fight against his hold. I want to scream at him to drop me, let me go. But something inside begs me to stay right where I am, testing his strength, pleading for him to conquer me with his body.

When his lips crash upon mine, I know what is happening. This is not a kind kiss – not one meant for your wedding altar or even the end of a date. This is the kiss of years of pent-up frustration. As his lips slide against mine and his tongue presses into my mouth, I realize this is the kiss of a man who thought he was dying only to find his lifesaving cure. And his cure tried to gaslight him into believing it was poison.

A moan escapes me, and he matches it with a growl. With his free hand, he guides my legs around him, and I feel the flex of his stomach beneath me. His harsh lips drop to the base of my neck, kissing and nipping up to the sensitive spot behind my ear, ripping unintentional noises from my throat. I try to bring my thoughts together to figure out how we got here, but I come up blank. His fang grazes my earlobe, and I completely forget we were fighting moments ago.

His voice is like heat in my veins, a low, rumbling whisper, "It seems you don't hear me unless I am rough, Sunshine. Must I be rough with you?"

"Yes," I breathe, catching his unexpectedly tropical scent all around me and the texture of a tree behind my back.

Kethi tsks. He braces me against the tree with his hips and tears my shirt down the center. The air is hot and muggy, still carrying the lingering heat from the late evening sun. So, there is no reason for tiny bumps to emerge across my skin except the brush of Kethi's callused fingers running down the center of my chest to the waistband of my pants.

He pauses, and I watch his eyes narrow and widen until the color overtakes them. Then, it's like we're back in full motion. His hot tongue runs over my nipple as his other hand tugs open my pants. I'm grateful for the minuscule breather I got because the moment his fingers graze my clit, my breath stalls in my chest.

"Breathe, Sunshine."

Choppy air enters my lungs. My chest stutters against him. He notches a knuckle against my clit, and his mouth wraps around my other nipple. My body bows against him, and Kethi brushes my clit before he moves his hand further down. I am an inexorable deluge beneath the belt, and the tilt of Kethi's lips confirms he can feel it.

"So wet for me," He whispers, his hot breath welcoming a new round of goosebumps along my neck and shoulder. He slides one finger inside me, and I can feel my pussy clench around him, "Responsive too."

He works his finger in and out, using his thumb against my clit, and I can feel myself grinding down against his hand. I'm an embarrassing cacophony of moans and mewls as he stiffens his thrusts, curling his finger against my g-spot.

"So vocal and yet," He thrusts a second finger inside me, "still no words."

He removes his fingers from my body, and I clench on air. I try to grind against him, and he leans away. A pitiful whimper sounds, and I curse internally when I realize it is mine. Kethi sets me down, and rejection threatens to sting through me.

"Take off your clothes, Sunshine."

Partially from embarrassment, partially from my underlying hint of rejection, I cross my arms over my chest instead.

Kethi's tongue brushes his lip before he catches it with his fang. My nipples are stiff peaks behind my arms, and I curse the day I landed on this planet. My body wants him more than my mind wants respect.

"Take off your clothes, Roxie." He says, leaning over me like the massive beast he is.

My fumbling fingers listen against the will of my mind. Starting with my holster, I toss it away before stripping off my pants. Most of the girls have been commando since we landed, but not me. Stripping out of the emergency tidy-whiteys from the pod, I stand naked before him.

His eyes are annoyingly bright with joy.

"They're off."

He smiles. Taking two Kethi-sized steps back, he orders, "Crawl to me."

I freeze. He's playing with me. He has to be. Then, he raises an eyebrow in my direction, and I'm on my hands and knees for some ungodly reason. Am I actually going to do this? Kethi's eyes go dark with lust, and I feel myself clench on air. Yeah, I want to do this, but my body won't move.

My logical mind is screaming at me, reminding me that I could say no at any point. Kethi is a gentleman, first and foremost, and he would stop this at the first sign of distress. I've never tested it, but I know he would. But for some reason, I've never been more turned on than I am right now at the challenge in his eyes.

So, as sensually as I can, I crawl. Kethi's not far, mere steps away. The ground is warm and squishy with pink moss, and he can't take his eyes off me. His eye color seems to ricochet back and forth as I move, staying glued to me. "That's my girl," He rumbles.

When I reach his feet, I don't wait for more orders. I come up on my knees, sliding my hands up his thighs and going for his laces. My arms are above my head, but I pay our size difference zero mind as I grip his massive cock.

My first thought is – *there's no way that's going in my body*. My second thought is – *if you can handle crash-landing on an alien planet, you can handle an alien dick*. Like a magnet within myself, I call together all the bravery it took to make every reckless choice I've ever made, and I draw a line with my tongue from the base of his cock all the way to the head.

His subsequent groan soothes my insecurities as I swirl my tongue over the head of his cock. It's hard and smooth but the same light blue as his skin. A thick silver vein runs across the underside, and when I slide a hand above his cock, reaching for his abs, I feel bumps and ridges I'd love to grind on. I wrap my lips around the head of his cock, and his hands fly to my hair, wrapping it in his fists and keeping me still.

I crawled, but he was not in control here. I resist his hold, lowering my mouth further onto his cock and hollowing my cheeks. My name is a plea on his lips as I peek at him through my lashes. His eye color is blown wide, and the muscles in his arms are straining as if he's holding himself back from roughing me up. That won't do.

I bring out all the stops, every trick I ever learned from a sexy magazine or the locker room talk of men in a military drill camp. I moan at his taste, breathe through my nose, and grip the base tightly in my hands. Until he's practically shuttling down my throat, face-fucking me with a look of pure disbelief on his face.

Still, I'm Roxie and Sunshine in his words, but he's thrown in pleas to Sheva, called me goddess and angel. I'm humming around his cock with every word of praise until he pulls out of my mouth. His cock pulses in front of me, and I expect him to come, but he doesn't. It bobs with the flex of his muscles, and he catches his breath.

"Tell me what you want, Sunshine."

He's back to commanding me. He's back to forcing us to talk when letting our bodies do the talking is easier. I want to glare, but I don't. He cups the side of my face, waiting patiently even as his body strains, and the sheer tenderness of the moment eases my resistance.

"I want you to fuck me, rough, against the tree like you've wanted since we first got tossed out into the woods together." I watch his reaction before adding, "Please."

CHAPTER THIRTY-FOUR
Kethi

I kneel over my *ĝha* and capture her lips with my own. Thanks to her ministrations and words, I am so hard I can feel the ache in my fangs. Still, I tease my *ĝha*'s body until she is begging and dripping for me. I only intend to be exactly as rough as I need to get Roxie to hear me.

I slide my cock against her little dot of pleasure at the apex of her thighs before I line my cock up with her center. Her whimper makes me smile. With one hand wrapped around my cock and the other braced beneath her hips, I guide my cock into her heat, slow and controlled.

When I'm seated inside her, I pause to let her adjust, but she does not wait. Roxie rolls her hips, grinding herself across my *b'atu* and moaning my name.

"That's right, Sunshine. Take your pleasure from my cock." My tone is reverent, and I'm certain this is the closest to divinity I've ever been. Watching my *ĝha* grind herself upon me, chasing her peak – I groan.

My hands wrap around her hips, and I drag my cock all the way out to the tip before slamming back into her. She is beautiful beneath me. Slim strands have fallen from the ball of hair at her neck, framing her pale face. She parts her lips with a moan as I slam into her again.

"Harder," She begs, sending pure male satisfaction through my body. I thrust harder, gripping tighter on her feminine hips. Her cunt grips my cock so right that I can feel the drag of her inner walls against me. She rolls her hips at the end of each thrust, and I feel her shiver of pleasure. I thrust again.

"Is that hard enough for you, Sunshine?"

Through half-lidded eyes, a slight smirk tilts her lips, "Harder."

I slam my cock into her again, pulling her hips and thrusting at the same time.

"Harder?" I ask, watching all her body's reactions.

"Harder," She confirms on a pant, rolling her hips again.

I follow her orders, giving it my all, meeting her circular grind at the end of the thrust.

"Yes, Kethi. Yes." She breathes, closing her eyes. She tilts her head back, baring her throat.

With each punishing stroke, her volume rises. With each thrust as her pleasure grows closer, but there is something I need to reach our peak with her.

"Eyes on me, Sunshine."

Her eyes snap open, meeting mine in the dark. Sensual little waves crest across her skin with my next thrust, her pointed nipples straining. She listens so well like this.

"You're mine, Sunshine." I thrust. "Do you know why?"

Her brows furrow, but she nods. My hips snap forward again.

"Tell me why, Roxie." The muscles in my arms bulge as I hold back my pleasure, waiting to hear her words.

"You're my mate, my *ĝha*." I thrust hard enough to turn her words into moans.

"And do you know what that means?"

"Tell me."

"It means you're mine." Thrust.

"Mine to love." Thrust.

"Mine to protect." Thrust.

"Mine to pleasure." Thrust. Thrust. Thrust.

"But most importantly, that means I'm yours too."

She nods, "You're mine."

"I'm yours, Sunshine. Forever."

She comes, spasming around my cock and ripping me over the edge with her.

Tucking her against my chest, I roll onto my back, removing her from the forest floor. With a gentle hand, I rub soothing circles up and down her back, brushing away broken tree needles and dirt.

Her voice is sleepy when she murmurs, "I didn't take you for a cuddler."

Hoping she hears it, I tell her through the bond, *"I'll be whatever you need."*

CHAPTER THIRTY-FIVE
Roxie

Every inch of my sex-drugged body chills to ice when I hear a snap of a twig and a low growl. *How could I forget we were in the freaking woods?*

"Kethi," I whisper, nudging his shoulder. He'd closed his eyes a minute ago and was apparently so blissed out he fell asleep – in the *woods*. Never mind that I was right there with him.

He grumbles slightly, and the growling grows louder. Cursing under my breath, I untangle myself from Kethi's arms and scan the darkness for my gun. The moon, which had been full days ago, was already fading in brightness, and with the trees blocking out the majority of its light, my human eyes were failing me. None of that would matter if I had my clothes on. There's a glow crystal in my pocket and a glowing dot on my front sight.

Where the hell is my gun?

The low rumbling growl is getting closer, and I pat the ground frantically like Velma, looking for her glasses. Jinkies.

Cool metal touches my left pinky, and I grab the weapon, feeling it unlatch from the holster. When I'm sure it's pointed away from me, I rest my finger beside the trigger guard. Whatever is out there won't be coming near me.

"Kethi," I whisper-shout, begging in my heart of hearts he will wake up from his place behind me. I have no clue how long we've been out here at this point, but the darkness is thick, and my eyes won't adjust right. I'm pointing my gun at every shadow like it's an enemy, and I can't tell fact from fiction.

Another crunch comes from my left, and I squeeze my eyes shut, opening them to the darkness again. The shapes of the trees seem to stand out, but Kethi is nowhere to be seen.

Since he was nearly ten feet of bright blue, you would think he'd be at least a little reflective, but I can't find him anywhere.

Without his voice in my ear or his warmth behind me, I start to lose sight of where I am. Am I in the woods? Or was it all a dream? Am I waking up in some underground bunker? Am I back on the *SS Herculean*? I try to take an inhale and focus on smelling the forest around me, but I can't stop panting. I'm forcing breath in through my mouth, but it won't fill my lungs right.

Another crunch comes, and a squelch. Vomit presses at the back of my throat as I see the carrion from the ship. More bodies are ground underfoot by chitinous legs. I step back from the sound, keeping my gun readied, aimed at the ground.

A chitter happens to my left, but another step comes from my right. Suddenly, a bright silver eye flashes through the area. In the moments before I'm blinded, something lunges for a mass of blue skin, and I shoot. Fifteen bullets.

The loud crack of my gun splits the silence of the night, sending off an echo reaching the end of the chain of events I started.

"Sheva, curse me." Kethi's voice comes.

No. No. No. No. No. Leaves rustle, and sound abounds. A glowing crystal lights the space, and Kethi fumbles for his bow. He is covered in some liquid, and I pray it's not blood as I follow his eyes to the animal in the brush. My eyes widen.

Bigger than any Earth wolf, the creature stands on four clawed paws and reaches Kethi's shoulders with its own. As if it wasn't scary enough from sheer size, as if it needed more defenses, black, shiny spines perk up between the fur around its back. Its calculating yellow eyes have locked on my *ĝha*.

I look back at Kethi, who has nocked an arrow but can't seem to draw it back, and I confirm he's bleeding. His muscles reject his movement as he tugs on the string, and I know what to do.

"Eyes or chest?" I ask, training my eyes back on the beast.

Kethi grunts with pain, and it's like I can feel it myself. My shoulder burns, and the fierceness of his anger alights in my blood.

"Do I shoot him between the eyes or the chest?"

Chest. It's not spoken, but it's clear as day. I should shoot for the heart.

As if the creature heard the answer, he wasted no time. Kethi can't pull the bow, and the scent of his blood has reached me. Metallic like a human's and yet more obviously his. Some primal part of me recognizes it. The primal beast in front of me realizes it too. He lunges for him.

I shot three times, aiming for its heart. Fourteen. Thirteen. Twelve. The beast looks like it will rake its claws down the front of Kethi before crumpling right in front of him, dying with a pained roar. Kethi looks from its glassy eyes to mine, and that's when I notice the third, silver eye staring back at me from his forehead.

CHAPTER THIRTY-SIX
Kethi

Roxie is the fiercest of *ĝhajo*, with the fiercest of weapons. But Sheva curse me; the tiny bullet buried in my shoulder burns. My *jisa* throbs and itches as it tries to heal the wound, unsuccessfully.

The growl of the *ùri nò* was loud enough to wake me, and I tried to be silent as I snuck behind it, allowing Roxie the time to find her weapon. I tried to use my third eye to attract her attention to the beast, but it only caused her to attack me with her tiny, damaging weapon. Thank the Baso Sheva, she could kill it herself.

"Shit. You're bleeding." Roxie says, rushing to my side. The low glow of the crystal light makes the blood from my wound look much worse. She's wearing her pants, and she's shredded her shirt further. She tied the small part that remained on her chest while pressing the excess fabric against the hole in my shoulder. "How much can *V`òllø* bleed?"

My head feels like it's filled with fluff, and I shrug my shoulders – or rather, I shrug my uninjured shoulder while the other sends stabbing pain from elbow to ear for trying to move it. My grunt of pain in unfortunate because it sends fear through my *ĝha*.

"I have more," I assure her, ignoring the wooziness. My third eye is still open, refusing to close even though the various auras and colors overstimulate my mind. Under its gaze, Roxie is lustrous. A hot pink aura radiates out from her body, colliding with the dark blue of my own. I give her a sleepy grin, and she shakes her head with disapproval.

Somehow, someway, I feel in my hearts that this is good, but I cannot imagine how. My *ĝha* hit me with her weapon. My *jisa* could not even stand against the tiny *bullet*. Yes, that is what she calls them when she counts them. Stinging, burning *bullets*.

"You're the most beautiful of lights, Sunshine," I murmur, reaching my good hand to hold hers against my chest. Her eye circles roll about their sockets.

"I'm going to get help. Keep this pressed against the wound." Roxie says, gathering herself. She takes the glowing crystal and pockets her gun as she glances around the woods. She looks up at the sky and sighs. "Which way to Valkarra?"

"We will go together," I insist, using my good arm to rise from the ground. Another gush of blood oozes from my shoulder, soaking through the remnants of Roxie's shirt, and I see her face pale. My legs feel heavy and weak, but I take tentative steps to prove I am still strong enough to hike out of the mountains. I look at the dead *ùri nò*. "We need to bring the beast."

Roxie whirls on me, "Are you serious? There's no way."

"I can carry it on my good shoulder," I say, unsure if that is true. Sunshine confirms my worst fears with a sharp shake of her head.

Her tiny eyes widen further. "Absolutely not. You can't even stand, Kethi."

"They will not accept us back into the village without it," I explain. A sharp pain goes through my head as her aura flares.

"Can we not bring a quill or ear or something?"

"We must bring the whole beast. As proof of the kill."

My *ĝha* groans in frustration, and the sensation grates through my body. My injured shoulder throbs, and I see her wince. Our connection is stronger already.

"I'll make a sled. Keep pressure on your wound."

I nod but fear for myself and my *ĝha*. Aside from the broken nose earlier this year, I'd only seen this much of my deep blue blood once in my life. It was before my *jisa* had fully developed, and it nearly killed me. Seeing it in this quantity, feeling my energy drain as I try to heal, is concerning, to say the least. And my third eye still will not close.

"Stay close," I try to command, but it comes out slurred.

"I will."

Roxie disappears behind a tree, the glow of her crystal follows, and I am alone again. I press the soaked rag against my wound, praying under my breath to Baso Sheva, but my eyes are growing blurry. My mind grows fuzzier. I can feel my strength draining from my body. I close my sight eyes and rest until my *ĝha*'s piercing scream wakes me.

CHAPTER THIRTY-SEVEN
Roxie

This is worse than war. Worse than the hospital. Worse than the ship because this feels hopeless. Somehow, I have to drag a three-hundred-pound alien and his ceremonial wedding kill out of an unfamiliar forest at night so he doesn't bleed to death because of me.

"Know your target." How many times was I told? How many times was it drilled into me? All for me to forget it now? I hear my father's voice in my mind; *you can't control the past, my little fighter.* But I can control how I react.

I promised Kethi I wouldn't stray too far, and our tiny impromptu camp was already out of sight. *Stay focused.* Branches. I need some sturdy branches. Unfortunately, most branches here are covered in those pointy needles, and I don't have time to strip them. So, I find ones I consider strong enough and begin to search for back supports.

My mind is a whirlwind as I search. There's no way they would turn away their injured king, right? If it comes down to our kill or Kethi, I will pick Kethi every single day. Surely his people would too. *Focus.*

I find one branch that looks wide and strong enough a little further up the hill and hike toward it. The glow of the crystal helps me see about twenty feet into the shadows, and the stick is at the edge of the light's touch. As my hand comes to a tree to support me, I hear another set of crunching steps and immediately swing my light around. A tiny bunny-like thing springs back into the shadows, and I take a deep breath.

Everything is fine. Maybe I could kill the bunny, and we could bring that back to Valkarra instead. I could strap the poor fluffy creature to my belt, and we could forget about the porcu-wolf hybrid haunting my lived experience. This seemed like a good enough idea that I hiked a few steps toward where I last saw it, grabbing the third sturdy branch. I keep my eyes peeled for the little creature when I crest a hill and enter a clearing. Feet away, the ground drops into darkness, but it doesn't matter because another mass glows in the distance.

A familiar round rock as wide as a bus glows from the center of a crater. It's black and porous with an eerie green glow and a million holes big enough for the creatures I last saw crawl out of one. Creatures with armored spider's legs and scaley green torsos. Creatures that refused to die even as I emptied round after round against their chest, neck, and eyes. Creatures with the intelligence to corrupt the files of the *SS Herculean* and capitalize on a full-scale evacuation.

My body chills, goosebumps creeping over my arms. I can't move. I can't reach for my gun or lower my hand from the tree supporting me. My legs won't move, and my breaths won't deepen. My eyes scan the area, searching for any hint of the monsters. And I can't stop the scream from escaping when they land on a pair of rigid legs resting against the glowing stone.

A large hand wraps around my mouth, and panic seeps into my bones. With my eyes squeezed closed in terror, I'm not sure how I can tell it's not Kethi, but it's not. This alien is smaller and lighter but just as strong. I force myself to open my eyes and see the arm holding me up. It's a warm brown color with geometric teal tattoos. It looks so human; I relax.

"I'm going to remove my hand now. Do not scream," A deep voice orders. "It makes them more active."

I nod against his hand, and he carefully steps back, releasing me. My gun is in my hand before I whirl on the guy, holding it up toward him. At the sight of him, my gun is lowering. Wings, the same color as his tattoos, reach out from the man's back, blending with the shadows of the dark.

His voice is quiet when he says, "You're one of the heavenly women."

I'm so discombobulated by the events of the night that I don't even bother to correct myself when I retort, "No. I'm Kethi's *ĝha*."

Not Commander Roxie Holt. Not Rox. Not even Sunshine. Kethi's *ĝha*. What in the actual f –

"Kethi Rogeshu?"

"Obviously." I tilt my head in agreement, remembering his lack of a translator.

The guy crosses his arms over his chest, and that is when I realized he's shirtless with *ĝha* marks of his own, diagonal across each pec. Yet, a cloak hangs around his neck, tucked in the center of his massive wings.

"Where is he? He would not let his *ĝha* wander this far into our territory. Certainly not close enough to *àĉhøale* abyss."

One of his words does not translate quite right, but it seems a fitting name for the crater beneath us – agony catastrophe. Now, how do I explain myself? How do I get him to help?

Before I can decide against it, I grab the man's hand. With one final look at the crater beneath me, I shudder. Tucking my sturdy branches under my arm, I drag him down the hill. As I force our way through the trees, heading in the direction I came, the sky begins to lighten to that familiar, ugly green.

"Roxie Holt," I say, pressing my hand holding the light against my chest. "You?" I point to him.

"Roxie? Your name? They call me Ijigan."

"Ijigan," I repeat, letting him know I understood him. "Kethi is this way," I point in the direction we are heading. He nods, but I'm not sure he understands. I want to explain how he's injured, and I need his help to get him and the beast back to Valkarra. I want to explain all that has happened, but I end up hoping Kethi is conscious when we arrive.

I lead Ijigan along a little faster and hope it won't be too late.

CHAPTER THIRTY-EIGHT
Kethi

My body feels buried in clay, and I cannot press it up from the ground, even as my core shouts at me to find my *ĝha*. Her piercing scream cut through the trees, only to be silenced, and I could not feel her on the other end of the bond. So, I must move, but my body will not.

Through gritted teeth, I grunt as I drag one foot beneath me, bracing my back against the tree. *You are Rogeshu. You will move.* I tow my other foot forward, keeping my hand pressed to the bleeding wound in my shoulder. Then, I stand.

Everything hurts down to the point where my hair meets my head. I manage three shuffling steps before leaning against another tree, and the world is spinning. Blood soaks my chest and pants, and I can't tell if it's all from my shoulder or if I am sporting multiple wounds. The entire front of my body is shining and blue with my blood, and I wonder if I will recover.

You are Rogeshu. You will survive.

"Roxie," I yell, though it comes out barely a whisper. "Roxie," I fail again.

Forcing myself further in the direction I last saw her, I look back at the glassy-eyed beast. Light is beginning to envelop the sky, and soon enough, the heat of the sun will be upon us. Even if I must drag that beast, rotted, into the village for our *r̈uṣad'ù* to be considered blessed, I will. Then, I remember my *ĝha* is hurt out there.

I make it another few steps and feel a sticky drop of blood slide down my forearm and drip from my elbow. The previous color of Roxie's shirt is completely covered in my dark blue blood, making me nauseous. This is definitely bad.

"Roxie," I try again.

I'm still within sight of our makeshift camp when she comes tumbling out of the woods. She turns away from me, looking at a Nusosan man – Ijigan, it seems. Her voice feels like miles away.

"He's injured." She says, but it feels like a dream.

Ijigan sees me, his own eyes sparking with concern at the sight of my blood. Then, the world fades to black.

CHAPTER THIRTY-NINE
Roxie

Never, never, never ask if it could get any worse. It can. It will. And today, it did. Kethi was up and *hiking* with a gunshot wound, calling my name in a pitifully quiet voice. Now, he's collapsed on the ground with his horn stuck under a tree root, and an idiot with wings is *yanking* him out.

Meanwhile, I strap together a stretcher for the dead porcu-wolf that both Kethi and Ijigan swear I need to be welcomed back into Valkarra. Apparently, I not only landed on an alien planet with divinely picked mates, magic tattoos, and wedding hunts, but I also landed on a planet willing to excommunicate its king and leave him to die if he doesn't have a *kill* from his wedding hunt.

Ijigan gets Kethi unstuck and slings him into his arms, bridal style, flinging drops of sapphire blood from my *ĝha*'s body. It sets my teeth on edge to see the graying spaces on his skin, and I can feel tears prick my eyes. Vera swore we would all be able to handle our *r̈ uṣad'ù*, and I want to punch her in the face for lying.

I get the animal strapped up, then Ijigan and I set off toward Valkarra.

The first sliver of the sun makes it over the peak of the mountains, lighting the forest below. I tuck away the glowing crystal and double down on my efforts to get down the mountain. It was a day's hike up, but the way Kethi's arm hung limply from Ijigan's embrace had me determined to make it down the mountain in half of the time.

Sweat is dripping off my forehead. It plasters my hair to my neck, and my shoulders ache from dragging the dead beast behind me. Aside from the occasional hangup on a wayward root or patch of moss, we're making good time. Still, I beg Kethi's higher power that he will be okay.

Along our journey, I consider dumping my gun here in the forest, never to see it or feel the press of guilt again. But then, I remember why I screamed, why Kethi was probably up and whispering my name. The monsters from the ship are here. Ijigan practically confirmed that the rock was a major catastrophe for his people too. I try to dislodge the thoughts invading my mind. Kethi is hurt because of me, and I must get him help.

We follow a sharp incline down until I can almost see the bright, crystalline domes of the Valkarran city. We come around a bend, and it's there. Just down the hill is the landing ledge, and less than a half mile further is the curving river of Valkarra, cutting its way through the picturesque buildings.

As we get closer, I see the human women huddled together, arguing with Serkha, and I call out for them.

My voice is raw when I yell, "Priscille! Erja! Clara!"

They all turn at the sound of my voice, dragging along a few younger *V`òllø* men to meet us on our path.

"Healer. We need a healer." I rasp. Erja nods in understanding, running down the hill to find someone to help. Serkha sees Kethi's limp body, and she makes it across the trail in seconds, her eye color widening with every passing step.

"What happened?"

"It was an accident." I scramble, trying to remember my military training. "We were resting when the sun went down when we were ambushed by this beast. Kethi tried to help me find it in the dark, and my bullet missed the target, hitting his shoulder instead."

Now, I'm actually sobbing. Actually breaking down. "He said we couldn't come back without the p-p-porcu-wooolf."

Tears spill over, cutting warm paths down my face as I sniffle. Priscille wraps her arms around me, and I collapse against her.

"He needs to be near the crystals." Serkha orders, demanding Ijigan fly him there. She looks at my sobbing face, and her eye color narrows. "Get up."

I cry harder but force myself to my feet. Priscille is there, keeping me steady with an arm while Clara listens intently, one step behind her.

Serkha grabs both of my arms, yanking me closer to her and out of Priscille's grip as her horns reach dangerously close to my face. "This is what is going to happen. You will go to the temple to sit with my son and strengthen him. You are *ĝharogeshu,* and you are strong and healthy. He is Rogeshu. He is the *King* of Valkarra, and he has a mighty *ĝha* sent by the Baso Sheva themselves. He will heal by your will."

I nod, only mildly bolstered as Serkha orders them to bring me to the temple. If Kethi lives, I will never argue about the legitimacy of our relationship again. If Kethi lives, I will proudly call him my *ĝha.*

But when I see him laid out on a crystal slab, with the fingers of the healer in his bullet wound, I'm not so sure he will live at all.

CHAPTER FORTY
Kethi

I can feel her there, but it's like there is a wall between us. My soul is floating in a different space than hers, a sliver out of reach. Yet, I'm drawn toward her, over and over. She feels like sunshine on my skin. Skin as cold as ice.

"If you can hear me, you better wake up." It's *her* voice, but as if we're both underwater. It carries like the voice of the *korovò*. They gave me some important advice recently, but I can't remember what they said.

"I'm serious, Kethi. You can't go making human women fall in love and then die on them. It's not gentlemanly. It's tragic and unfair, and I've had enough tragedy and unfairness in my life."

Human. It's such an odd word, but it tickles something in my mind. A short woman with long black hair and warm eye circles that stay the same size even when she is mad. She has tiny hands but a big attitude, and she respects me. She trusts me, I think.

"You need to wake up. You need to say, 'It will all be okay, Sunshine.' You need to kiss your ĝha and finish our wedding so we have a legal reason to never be apart."

My *ĝha* – I have a *ĝha*. She keeps calling to my soul. She keeps me from staying here, wherever 'here' might be. My *ĝha*.

Sunshine.

"Roxie."

CHAPTER FORTY-ONE
Roxie

An entire week goes by without him waking up. I try everything. I move his body around, keeping him comfortable and babbling about a hundred different topics. I tell him about the crater, and how the same aliens hiding out there are the ones who killed the people of the *SS Herculean*. Soon after, I decided traumatic stories won't help him wake up, so I changed the subject and stuck with funny or cute stories from my childhood. I told him about the musical numbers my sister and I would choreograph and how my dad was a big fan of Halloween. When that didn't work, I transitioned to funny stories to inspiration. I wanted to give him a reason to wake up. I needed him to wake up. So, I started making promises.

I promised to kiss him daily, even if I was mad at him. I promised him I would create a cute nickname for him like he has for me. His finger twitched when I called him K-Star, and I promised him I would try it out for real if he woke up. I promised Kethi I would keep his room clean and make his bed so he had a clean place to come back to. I even tried to tempt him out of his unconsciousness by promising to crawl for him again.

When he didn't wake up after all that, I turned to demands. They were what I did best. It's what my team on Earth believed. It's what the guys on the ship joked about with me. I always fell back on demands when I felt out of my depth. So, I started demanding he wake up and do something.

That was why I squeaked like a bird when his untried voice whispered, "Roxie."

I had never moved so fast in my life. Kneeling by the tiny bed they dragged into the temple, I clasped his hand in my own.

"I'm right here."

Under the glow of the crystals reflecting off the temple's stone walls, Kethi squeezed my hand back for the first time in a week. His eyes opened partially but were drained of color. His skin still held a terrifying silver pallor. But he was okay. He was breathing. He was saying my name.

"You're real," He murmurs sleepily, his fang peeking out of the left side of his mouth tilts up.

I curl up close on his good side. "Real as it gets."

He squeezes me closer to him, and relief floods me on the cellular level. He's already stronger. The shiny shield along his skin seems to be in hyperdrive because it's knit tightly across his skin.

"Were you worried about me, Sunshine?"

I scoff. I was terrified, but I would never give Kethi the satisfaction. "Of course not. You're my *ĝha*. You would never leave me."

Death didn't care what we believed. But I refused to acknowledge the alternative – that my stupid human weapon could have killed the only alien on this planet who is vital to me. That *I* could have killed someone important to me. I couldn't even touch it to count my bullets while he was out. I left it beside our bed when I went for my jumpsuit.

"It was dumb of me to jump in front of your *bullet,* huh?" He jokes, using his injured arm to stretch my leg over him.

"The dumbest," I whisper, cuddling into his side. I can feel the tears pricking at my eyes again, and I bury my face against his chest so he won't see.

"I could never leave you, Sunshine. Even in the after, you were there, guiding me home to you."

"Always with the words," I mumble, feeling a tear breach my lower lashes. Kethi chuckles, brushing a hand over my hair.

The relief that he is okay exhausts me. All the fight I've been holding onto since I landed on Shojo seems to drain from my body. And where I expected floods of anxiety, there's a feeling of comfortable paralysis. I couldn't move from this spot if I wanted to, but I don't want to. I would actively argue against moving from this spot.

"Sunshine?" Kethi asks, his voice low in my ear.

"Hm?"

He growls playfully, pinching my side. "I thought we already talked about you using your words."

I roll my eyes, "Yes, Kethi? My *ĝha*, my mate, my K-Star?"

"K-Star?" I peek up at his face and giggle at his confusion. Definitely not the fitting nickname for him. "You were going to ask me something."

He seems to come back to himself. He relaxes into the bed, resuming the soft circles on my back. His eyes glance around the cavern, and with a serious voice, he asks, "Is that my sister, or am I still under the effects of lifesaving herbs?"

I glance behind me, and lo and behold, Xatsoe has returned. And she's glaring right at us.

CHAPTER FORTY-TWO
Kethi

It does not take long to remember I am alive and full of responsibility once my sister enters the room. Given my healing, I assume we managed to get the beast down the mountain. I also imagine I have been asleep for quite a time to garner this cling from my strong and independent *ĝha*.

"Xatsoe, great to see you," I say as Liro enters behind her, catching his breath as if he had been running.

"I told her you were still not recovered," My brother explains. Roxie groans, burying herself further into my side.

Upon seeing my sister, I easily overlook her unhappiness. Xatsoe is unhappy? Not unusual. I'm sure she will be expanding upon her frustrations with me soon. And since she was in Wupeso, I imagine she has plenty to say about how terrible of a brother and Rogeshu I am. I'm sure it was a terrible time in the village, and she can't wait to tell me. So, I wait for her to speak. To share what is burning in her mind.

"You send me away," She starts, coming a step closer. "And then you almost die?"

I chuckle, which only seems to incense her further. "I came nowhere near death. My body needed time to recover from copious blood loss. Isn't that right, Sunshine?"

"Yes," She groans. I feel a twinge of guilt through our bond but soothe it with strength and forgiveness. I think some tension is released from her body, but she does not say anything about it.

"Brother, if you die, what is to happen in Valkarra? I cannot be Rogeshu. I will never be ready to be Rogeshu."

So this is her concern. My sister was afraid for her negotiated freedom, not necessarily my well-being. I intend to tell her this, but her horns fall, and she adds, "If you die, what will happen to our family? We need you like we needed our father."

"Xattie, I would not have died," I assure her. "Now, I am healthier than I have ever been. Look at my *jisa*." I motion to the tight weave of light, the extra concentration on my shoulder as it finishes healing the injury.

Unfortunately, even Liro looks a little pale. And when my mother enters the room behind them to see me awake and speaking, the truth of my condition sinks in. I was much closer to the deities than I initially thought. I look down to Roxie to ask her about it, but soft snores snuffle against my side. I wonder if she slept at all while I was out.

My mother is quiet when she says, "The human intelligence, Blossom, would like to come to check on you. She has been helping the healers with your care."

With a tilt of my horns, I approve, and the pinkish-gold humanoid enters the temple. Her lavender eyes scan the crystals, taking in information and making vocal notes for later. She gives me an odd smile when she approaches, and I force myself into a seated position.

The unlucky side effect is that Roxie wakes up. She sees my family gathered, and Blossom, and the tension returns to her shoulders with practiced ease. Roxie gives them all a tight smile as she detangles herself from me and stands from the bed. At some point, one of the human women must have brought her jumpsuit because she wears it now. With her hair twisted into a low bun at the back of her head, she pushes her shoulders back and waits attentively as Blossom scans my body.

"Your wound healed. Your *jisa,* the protective organ most damaged by the bullet, recovered – recharged. May I take a sample of blood from your finger?"

I hold my hand out to her, and she stabs a tiny metal needle into it. I'm impressed with its strength, as it seems to puncture through my *jisa* without issue. But, when I look closer, I see that the jisa has actually moved around the tiny metal pin. The small dot of blood disappears, and whirring sounds follow.

"Your connective bond with Roxie remains strong. Though, given the comparative sample of blood to your brother, you may continue to feel weakened for the next day – sun cycle."

"He will not die?" Xatsoe asks.

"Correct. He will not die from these injuries." Blossom confirms.

The collectively held breath in the room releases, and Roxie nods. Without turning away from the room, she addresses me to tell me she needs to debrief with Blossom. Before I can heave myself out of bed or follow her, she disappears with the golden girl around the corner.

CHAPTER FORTY-THREE
Roxie

Embarrassment, guilt, relief, and exhaustion are only a few of the feelings clogging up my mental clarity when I rush from the temple. Blossom is right behind me as I keep my clipped walk. Gone is the Roxie who shot an evil alien on the ship, felt like some Lara Croft badass, and introduced herself to a pod full of freaked-out women like a cocky space cowboy, only to be replaced by the Roxie who is two shakes from a panic attack because she shot a good alien on a friendly planet like an untrained redneck with a cold six-pack down.

Once outside the temple, I can feel the cool breeze from the river wafting through the air. I wring my hands in front of me, reaching for my gun only before remembering I left it back at Kethi's house with my dirty clothes. I didn't want it near me until I knew he would be okay.

"I know I've already asked these questions, but it didn't nick his heart? There is no internal bleeding?"

"From all my scans, I assure you it did not puncture either *V`òllø* heart. It tore through Kethi's shoulder muscles which are structured similarly to human shoulder muscles."

"You swear it wasn't the gun that caused most of the damage?"

"As I told you before, *V`òllø* have two hearts. This means they pump twice as much blood through their system, twice as fast. Thanks to their *jisa,* they do not often bleed. But since the gun pierced his *jisa* at the shoulder, it was not protecting his legs when the beast's claw scraped across the artery."

Guilt eats me from the inside out. "I don't know how I missed the leg injury. How Ijigan missed it."

"There was a lot of blood on his clothes. Even the healers did not see it until the bullet wound was closed."

"Now you appeal to my sensibilities," I grumble. Blossom smiles.

"They designed me to keep the humans of escape pod three happy," She tells me.

"Is that true?"

"No."

Nerves eat at my stomach when I realize what I have to ask her about next. "Blossom, I have to tell you something."

"I am here to help."

"Out in the forest, I saw one of the rocks the aliens that attacked the ship came from. Do you know why they might be here?"

"I do not."

"Do you know *anything* about them that might be helpful? Ijigan said they are attracted to sound."

Blossom seems to stutter. Her left wrist twists before she answers, "No, I know nothing about *redacted.*"

My eyebrows shoot to my hairline. In training, they taught me they created Blossom to navigate the escape pods in case of emergency. She joked they made her to keep the escape pod occupants happy. Yet, we learned she was much more than an escape pod assistant since we landed. They equipped her with medical care information, the ability to process natural languages, interpersonal skills, and more. Truthfully, I didn't believe they kept a single ounce of data from the bot.

So, when the light from her eyes shuts off, and she goes still, I panic. Then, she starts up again and says, "Ask me again."

I do, but we get the same answer. They have redacted something in her system. Her natural response is edited for consumption, and that opens a whole host of questions. At one point, what information did she have that she could no longer share with the women under her care? That she can no longer communicate with a Commander of the *SS Herculean*? Does it have something to do with the siege? Or is it something innocuous the company wanted to protect?

"Did this happen from the corrupted file on the escape pod?" I ask, my confusion escalating near concern.

"What corrupted file?" She turns off and on once again. "Ask me again."

CHAPTER FORTY-FOUR
Kethi

I am greeted by King Solispera and his Mivonie, Ijigan, the moment I step out of the temple. The King is intimidating by himself, but with Ijigan beside him, I question my fortitude so soon after my blood loss. Never before would I have this lack of confidence, but my family and *ĝha* were full of fear for me.

It did not help that Roxie never returned. She sent Blossom in to let me know she would stay at my mother's house for the night and that I should go home to rest in my bed. As disappointed as I was to find I would not be sharing my bed with Roxie, it reminded me our r̈u̥sad'ù was not finished. Plus, my *ĝha* knows best, so I listened to her wisdom while my siblings fought over who would walk me home.

It infuriated Xatsoe when King Solispera dismissed her. Ijigan gave her an apologetic flutter of his wings, but it didn't soothe her. She returned his apologies with a vulgar gesture. Leaving me with the knowledge I would never understand their relationship.

"My hand informed me we found your soulmate near the abyss. You should have her inspected by the healers and the flower woman." King Solispera begins.

A spike of fear drives through my hearts, ripping a growl from low in my chest. I squelch it but maintain the information like a proper leader should. Clasping my hands behind my back, I walk toward my home with Liro behind me.

"Thank you for telling me."

"Of course, we would protect the Valkarran women as our own. Including any who take refuge from the stars."

This surprises me since the king of the Nusosan people is not known for his understanding and generosity. When he comes to Valkarra, everyone looks away, worried about attracting his ire, without knowing how much he does to protect them and our people. It is why I work away the mornings in my childhood role, creating tools and weapons for them.

"Are there any updates on the beasts of the abyss?"

King Solispera defaults to his hand, and Ijigan responds, "We have gathered no further information. From what we can tell, there are three of them, and they do not venture far from the abyss except to hunt."

"Did they see my *ĝha*?"

Ijigan looks me directly in the eyes when he says, "No. I ensured it."

Gratitude bubbles in my chest at his words. I remember feeling Roxie's hopelessness on the mountain, and then I felt nothing. At first, I worried she was dead, but suddenly I saw her on the hill, Ijigan behind her. I was further relieved when I woke up with her in my arms.

"All is well," I announce, feeling lighter already. With Liro behind me, I begin the trek to my home.

"If I may?" Ijigan asks, pausing me in my tracks.

"Always."

"Your *ĝha* seemed to know something about the rock. She was afraid before she ever saw the creatures."

"My blood flowed freely down the mountain. I'm sure her fear was my fault."

"Of course, I only meant she inspected the crater closely. As if she knew she may find something unsavory."

King Solispera tells his hand it is enough and assures me they have the abyss well-handled. But Ijigan achieved his objective. Concern knots inside me about my *ĝha*'s knowledge of the creatures of the abyss.

"Liro, what do you think?"

"You and your *ĝha* have survived a traumatic encounter blessed by Baso Sheva. You need rest to handle this new information."

The Nusosan King and Hand nod in agreement before letting me know they will be staying for the remainder of my *r̈uṣad'ù*. They congratulate me on our kill during the hunt, trying to distract me from the concern they've caused, but it does not work. As soon as they are away from me, I begin to work.

"Find Blossom and send her to our mother's home to inspect Roxie. Send the healer's as well. I will ask her about the creatures of the abyss at the first sliver of the sun."

"Kethi – "

"And announce the date of the temple ceremony. We will finish our *r̈uṣad'ù* tomorrow. Eight sun cycles are quite long enough."

"Kethi – "

"And find Roxie's weapon. She was not wearing it this evening, and I need to understand how it works. It is fierce and could be useful."

Liro stops walking with me. His eye color is pointed tightly in my direction. I stop with him. His color has paled, and his hands are shaking. His horns are dropped low.

"What is it, brother?"

"I am glad you are alive."

My hearts soften, and I step toward him. We tangle our horns, and he clasps my hands in his to stop their shaking.

"Me too, Liro. Me too."

CHAPTER FORTY-FIVE
Roxie

Since my *ĝha* is such a worrywart, it did not surprise me to find him in his mother's kitchen the following day. After sending Blossom to Serkha's house for an entire medical workup, I was surprised when he wasn't there last night to ensure I submitted.

"Hello, Sunshine." He says, ducking under his mother's crystal light fixture to kiss my forehead.

"Good morning, KK," I say, deciding KK for King Kethi was not the suitable nickname at that moment. Turning my attention to Serkha, I ask, "Did Kethi ever have a nickname growing up?"

"Liro called him *ghode*, and Xatsoe called him *ghono*, but both of those are poor, unlike his nickname for you."

From the translations in my ear, I would have to agree, so I throw them out with the other rejects. Since Kethi is here, Serkha already has a full breakfast spread across the table, and the scent of that sweet bread Kethi offered me on the floating island fills the room. I assume the smell drags Xatsoe from her bed before the sun has hit its first full sliver because she is half-asleep when she shoves a piece into her mouth. The crumbs scatter across the wood.

"Good morning, llosuhi." Kethi greets her, placing a kiss on her forehead.

Through a mouthful of *ur'e gu*, she mumbles, "*Ghono.*"

Serkha only rolls her eyes. When Liro joins us, I genuinely feel like an outsider. Dinner with them felt like the opportunity to break the ice, but Xatsoe was in Wupeso, and everyone was on their best behavior, it seemed. This was different.

Here and now, Serkha doted on her children. She guided them to their plates, filled their dishes with their favorites, forgoing the foods they obviously didn't like. While they chewed, she spoke of her expectations of them, mixing in praise for how proud they made her. She did the same for me when it was apparent that I wasn't sure where I fit in. From my place along the wall, feet from the table, she guided me next to Kethi. She put a plate of food together for me, avoiding all the sweet breakfast items, much to the family's chagrin. Still, she placed it in front of me and explained how happy she was to add me to the family and how excited she was to officiate our ceremony tonight.

It felt like an out-of-body experience like I was seeing the room from above. It didn't feel like it could be real. Commander Roxie Holt didn't belong on an alien planet with a beautiful alien soulmate and a new family. She was supposed to be waking from guilt-fueled nightmares in the middle of the night. She didn't deserve to have a new mother who remembered her food preferences and vocalized her pride. She had a mother on Earth, a mother she loved, who criticized her mercilessly and loved her just the same.

But it was real. It was real when Kethi smiled at her and kissed her cheek with his lips sticky from his favorite breakfast cake. It was real when Serkha reprimanded Liro and Xatsoe for fighting at the breakfast table. And when Xatsoe immediately finished her breakfast to crawl back into bed until the rest of them moved on for the day, that was real too.

"You know what I realized today?" Kethi asks me, placing my hand in the crook of his elbow as we walk through town.

"What?"

"You could have kissed me on the ship without breaking your self-proclaimed rules."

"Would that have changed anything?"

"No, but it would have been one more kiss, and I find that I wonder how I can win one more kiss often."

I smile because it's cheesy and ridiculous, and those seem to be two words I would use to describe Kethi in his entirety, right alongside strong, diplomatic, and intentional. I might include words like family man and protector. Or maybe less protector and more primal. I can protect myself.

"As much as I would hate to ruin those thoughts," He gives me a pointed look. "I need to ask you about the abyss. The Nusosans said you seemed to know of the creatures who live there."

I didn't expect the conversation to go in this direction, but I nodded. Images from the ship flood my mind, and I cringe when I can't reasonably avoid the memory of a man's head being stabbed through with a pointed leg. Kethi seems cowed because he gathers me closer to him.

We've somehow made our way to a bench beside the river. Behind us, farms are growing tall and colorful, and across the churning water, colorful mosaic murals decorate the walls. Whenever I pause long enough to truly see Valkarra, I'm reminded of its beauty – different than Wupeso and, in my opinion, more stunning by half. I keep my eyes locked on the water and deeply breathe into my belly.

"They attacked the *SS Herculean*. Only there were more, significantly more of that rock they make their ships from and more foot soldiers than I saw in the crater."

Kethi squeezes my hand in his, and I give him a tight smile.

"Do you know anything about them? Why they might be here? Their weakness?"

"The more I learn about them, the more terrifying they get. They're attracted to sound, according to Ijigan. My gun does nothing against their skin, though I did puncture one's eye. Their ships are made of the glowing rock, and they're more intelligent than I gave them credit for." A terrible thought invades my mind, "Are there more than the ones in the crater? Have they been *leaving* the crater?"

He shakes his head. "They only leave to hunt and never far. At least not yet."

CHAPTER FORTY-SIX
Roxie

As the women huddle around me, preparing my face with homemade makeup and practically sewing me into my dress, I think about the monsters and Kethi and Blossom's redacted information. Forget the blessing of being surrounded by my friends in my new mother-in-law's home, about to marry the best man I've ever met in my life. That man almost died and left me on a planet hosting some of the evil aliens of my nightmares.

Clara's hands are in my hair, and I'm reminded it's entirely too long with her finger combing. Meanwhile, Priscille paints my fingernails a pink color I never would have allowed pre-crash, and Erja is holding my chin still as she glues tiny crystal shards to the edge of my eye.

All around me, they speak of lighthearted topics. Priscille is telling us about Serkha's offer to join the next exploration. Clara speaks of King Solispera – or Sol, as she calls him. And Erja explains how kind the men have been toward Ian and how well they handle his overstimulation. They speak like I've been there the entire time, not off hunting in the woods or hiding on the island's ledge. They talk as if I know all the stuff I missed. And it makes my heart ache because their support has been there the entire time.

I feel the tears prick at my lashes, and Erja orders, "Roxie, no."

I snort, and one tear escapes, only to be caught on Erja's slim fingertip. She brushes it on her pants, and I thank a higher power for my friends. Guilt bites at me for keeping secrets from them. But could I tell them about the monsters? Would they still trust Blossom if they knew about the secrets she was keeping?

"Crying on your wedding day is good luck," Priscille says, finishing the final coat on my pinky. "Or at least that's what the abbess always said."

"Crying may be good luck, but looking as though you've cried is a first-class ticket to everyone believing you are marrying the bastard against your will," Erja touts.

"Erja!" Clara reprimands, dropping my hair across my back. The soft strands graze my bare shoulder blades, and I shiver. I hate that it can even touch my shoulder blades.

"Ladies, is there any way you could cut my hair?" I ask, redirecting the conversation. There are a hundred words I want to say and ask. I wonder if Erja knows much about marrying someone against her will and what other lessons the abbess taught Priscille. I wonder if Clara is enjoying Valkarra as much as we are. I wonder if they are all as strong as they seem and if they would handle the news of the monsters well.

"Yes. Of course." Priscille says.

"Someone hand me the scissors," Clara announces, and Priscille does. No one speaks. I don't move a muscle as Clara feels her way up to the perfect length and expertly makes the first cut.

I feel free the moment the first snip is over. A chunk of silky black hair floats to the floor, collapsing against the wood. Clara follows the line with her fingers and makes another cut and another until my hair sits in a sharp line right above my shoulders.

Erja wolf whistles. Priscille claps.

"I assume that means it looks good," Clara says, letting out a breath she must have been holding.

"It looks fantastic," Priscille responds.

"Just like Roxie," Erja adds.

I decided then and there that I couldn't keep secrets from them, especially not about the monsters or Blossom. We were in this together.

"Good," Clara announces, running her fingers through the strands several more times. "She's ready."

My voice isn't as strong as I hope when I say, "Not quite."

CHAPTER FORTY-SEVEN
Kethi

I look like my father. The shining surface before me reflects my father's image. Liro and Xatsoe see it, too. I can tell from the way they look at me. My traditional *r̈ uṣad'ù* clothing was fashioned after his, the tailor told me. Only mine was updated with the finest fabrics. In the end, the differences didn't matter because I looked exactly like him. The spitting image of Rexh Rogeshu.

I rub a hand down the front of my black tunic, feeling the exquisite embroidery of silver thread at the cuff. It's tucked into a fabric cage at my waist, with sharp boning and black crystals sewn in detailed patterns. Xatsoe guides the light gray, silky swath beneath it over my shoulder and through the metal adornment, letting it fall like a cloak across my back. Then, I am complete.

"You have never looked more like Rogeshu than you do today," My mother says, emotion swelling in her voice. "Your father would be most proud."

We tangle horns momentarily before Xatsoe forces her way into a tangle, and Liro follows suit.

As one not often taken with nerves, they feel unfamiliar when I consider my *ĝha* will be binding herself to me forever today. Somehow, we went from that fateful moment on the ledge, where she swore never to visit Valkarra, to here in a short time. All she has to do now is meet me in the temple, have the special words spoken over us, and accept our bond.

My mother guides me to the *r̈ uṣad'ù* chamber, and I try to catalog all the details before she wraps the blindfold over my sight eyes. Someone decorated the pews with flowers, and the glow of the crystal spires emanated throughout the space, bathing us in a soft golden light. When my eyes are covered, I imagine what Roxie might look like walking down the aisle toward me. I wonder if they will dress her in our custom or like she would have on Earth. I wonder if her hair will be up, like when she hikes or flies. Or if she will wear it down like she usually does. The longer I wait, the more I fear she will not show up at all, and I'm forced to take a steadying breath.

At the bottom of my exhale, my mother whispers, "She is here."

My ears perk when her steps reach them and again when they stop right across the aisle from me. My mother's words are quiet as she explains the blindfold to Roxie, and my heart leaps at Roxie's quick acceptance. Then the rest of our guests enter, and the crowd drowns her soft breaths out.

Soon enough, my cue comes to open my third eye, and I'm pleasantly surprised when it does so without issue. My breath is still stolen from my lungs at the image of Roxie through Baso Sheva's energy. She is surrounded in bright pink, and it's so distracting I almost miss the sharp protection of our *jisa* across her skin. Her aura is centered on her warm brown eyes, and even through my third eye, I can tell something is different about her.

My mother guides us through the sacred words, inviting the witnesses to bless us. I hear Kano and his *ĝha* among them, and relief for Liro's thorough nature swipes through me. My mother instructs us to connect our hands. The room quiets, and I can feel Roxie's mind open up to my own.

"Hey, Sunshine."

I can feel her unique blend of nerves and joy and how my nickname warms her.

"Hello, My King." She does not pause to embrace the way she makes me feel with her words – unstoppable. "Imagine my surprise when I run a hand through my freshly cut hair and notice my skin shimmer."

"You cut your hair?" My curiosity begins to imagine the many possibilities. Will I be able to see her tiny ears? Does it still reach her lithe shoulders?

"You'll see soon enough."

"According to my mother, we're supposed to be making promises. Exchanging promises." I remind her and myself.

"Well then, I promise to let you see my hair soon."

I am smiling, but the room outside us is still silent. "I think they're supposed to be more long-term."

"I don't see you making any promises, My King."

I ignore her thoughts of my smile and focus on all the promises I want to make. "How about this? You give me one good one, and I will give you mine."

"Hm," She teases, "I guess that will work. I promise you that I won't question our bond because I know this is as real as it gets."

I'm stunned silent when our bond severs, and the room's sounds rush back double time. My third eye was open, but an inky darkness emanating from the back drowned every aura in the room.

"Something is wrong," Roxie announces.

"Something is wrong." I agree, trying to see through the invading black.

"Finish your vows," My mother orders, a tense string of concern in her voice. "I can't cut the blindfolds until you finish your vows."

I don't hesitate, immediately jumping back into Roxie's mind and rattling off every promise I'd been preparing since I met her.

"We don't have time for – "

"These are my promises. I will always listen past your words to what you truly mean. And I promise to confirm what you mean with you. I promise to keep you close and ensure you feel your best. I promise to make sure your life here is full of thrills. You will always have a family with me. I'll protect you from your night terrors and the terrors of the night. And I promise I won't die if you injure me, and I won't leave you alone on my strange planet. But most of all, I promise to love you through monsters and myths and whatever is going on outside our bond."

"Wow. I wish we had time to unpack all that."

Our bond severs, my mother cuts our blindfolds, and chaos ensues.

CHAPTER FORTY-EIGHT
Roxie

This is bad. This is really bad. One of the scaley spider creatures is crashing through the entry of my wedding chamber. And Vera is here – all the human women are standing near me. They're protected by Wupesons and Valkarrans alike, but it doesn't matter because we've watched one of those creatures shred through hundreds of humans in minutes. And from the sapphire blood on the walls behind it, this temple has been no different.

I need my gun. The women need an alternate exit. We need heavier weaponry and for everyone to stop screaming. The screaming will only make it worse.

"Is there another exit?" I ask Serkha, taking her attention from her son – my *ĝha* – fighting his way in front of his people.

"No. Yes. It may not be safe."

"It's safer than here. Take the women, escape. Get them to safety."

I hear the whimper of a *V`òllø* woman toward the door, and my heart aches in my chest. I've got to find a way to stop this before –

A wet, sucking sound sends a familiar shiver down my spine. Vomit rises to the back of my throat, and I force myself to breathe. In case the sound effects weren't enough, I looked over in time to see the monster's leg exit a swiftly graying body. A *V`òllø* body.

Aston stifles a sob, letting Llazho push her further away from the monster. Vera gathers all the women, including the *V`òllø*, the same way she did on the ship, as I order, "Listen up, Serkha will get you out of here. Follow her."

Priscille's hand tightens on my arm. "Serka will get us out of here."

"I'll be right behind you," I agree, ripping my arm from her grip. She stares into my eyes with the power of God behind her because the guilt for my lies eats away at my soul. I whisper, "You would have made a great nun on Earth."

Serkha presses an old stone behind the dais, opening a tight exit they can squeeze through. Then, she and Vera work together to shuffle out the women. Erja holds Ian tightly, cradling the eight-year-old to her chest to block out the violent sounds and screaming. I express my thanks that the other children are with the *peholoe* in Wupeso and shove Priscille toward the line of exiting women. Serkha led the way, leaving Vera to take up the back, but I watched in horror when she didn't. She presses the stone button again, sliding the exit closed from this side and staying on this end of it.

Vera walks with a practiced ease when she meets me at the top of the steps.

"What are you doing?" We ask in unison as if we both believe the other stupid for staying.

"I can't leave my *ĝha*." We respond in kind. It's a tender moment for about point-two seconds before we hear another familiar sound of rending flesh, and our heads snap forward to ensure it's not our idiot lovers. It's not.

"Thank Baso Sheva," Vera whispers, and my eyes widen slightly. It's wild how fast conditions change around here. "So, what's the game plan, Commander?"

"Your guess is as good as mine."

"We need to stop the weapons they're walking on."

As I'm about to shout my order, three *V`òllø* men act on my same conclusion, Kano included. It seems to spur something in some of the others because they are only seconds behind until the monster is pinned down by its legs, gnashing its huge, Nosferatu-looking fangs in their direction.

"Their eyes are the only soft part of their bodies I could find," I explain.

"Tell your *ĝha*." Vera orders. As soon as I think about shouting it, Kethi's voice is in my mind.

"You have an idea, Sunshine?"

"Go for the eyes."

I expect him to plunge his hand in there or use a shard of broken pew. What I do not expect is for him to draw something black and metallic that looks suspiciously like my gun, point it straight at the creature's eye, and shoot it in an enclosed space.

The sound echoes around us, and I slam my hands over my ears, already hearing the ringing startup. The creature still isn't dead, so Kethi shoots out two more eyes at point-blank range.

With the second and third shots, I realize it is my gun. Somehow, Kethi has my gun, and it's still not working on the evil, creepy alien invading my wedding – and I'm three bullets shorter.

After three shots to the eyes, Kethi and I determine it's not working. He steps back as the others fight to control the monster's legs. With each damaging attack, the beast fights harder, snarling and throwing his body weight toward my *ĝha*.

Then, as I'm about to tell him to see if the creature has a soft underbelly, Vera's *ĝha* uses his strength to twist the creature's leg off its body. I catch sight of a fleshy glimmer attached to the bottom as it jerks in their hold. Kethi must see it, too, because as Kano goes for another leg, my *ĝha* slides beneath the creature, tossing away the weapon.

Moments later, the monster's body crumples and a fleshy green sack is thrown from beneath it. The legs go limp, and the men roll the creature off my *ĝha*, baring a gaping hole in the yellowish underbelly.

It covered Kethi in gore. His hands are drenched in black blood, while his chest is covered in spoiled green slime. The sack is mere feet away, twitching, and Kano squashes it under his boot as he walks for his *ĝha*, gathering Vera in his arms. The other *V`òllø* are already tending to the dead, and I remember I haven't moved from my spot.

Three bounding steps later, I throw my arms around Kethi without thinking about the mess. He easily hoists me into his arms, and I smack my lips to his.

"I am not injured." He assures me through our bond.

"Good, because our wedding night is far from over."

CHAPTER FORTY-NINE
Roxie

Our reception didn't happen for another few days. Instead, we made time for meetings and funerals. The Nusosan people had to be apprised of the new information, the Wupesons had to be introduced to the Nusosans, and funerals had to be held for the two fallen *V`òllø*. The women all made it through the secret exit fine, choosing to hide out on Serkha's ship in case they needed to evacuate from Valkarra, and when all was said and done, no one felt like celebrating. Until today.

Under a crystalline dome decorated in glowing lights, open to the air, human, *V`òllø*, and Nusosan alike dance and celebrate together. Everyone dressed in colorful finery, and our traditional Valkarran wear was clean and new. Ornate lamps hang above sandstone arches, casting shadowed flowers and shapes along the walls and drapery. Soft, melodic music fills the air, played on unfamiliar instruments and harmonized with deep *V`òllø* voices. They inspire movement and conversation among the people and hold me in complete awe.

"There's something I'd like to show you," Kethi whispers, sending shivers down my spine. He escorts me from the center of the decadent reception hall and into a quiet Valkarran street. The part of me who knows him is excited about his surprise, but the other is concerned about how people would react to our sudden disappearance.

"Can we leave our own reception like this?"

"We are the *ĝhajo*. We are Rogeshu. We can do whatever we please, especially tonight."

Kethi is entirely unbothered. His fangs are displayed in his signature grin, and it is impossible for me to fight him when he looks at me that way.

"Lead the way."

With my hand in his, he brings me through town, down shadowed roads, and away from the party. Since the entire village is celebrating our *r̈ ůṣad'ù*, this is the darkest I've seen the city. Even though the crystalline domes glow blue in the moonlight above us, the streets are dark. If I weren't with Kethi, I might even be nervous. But with my hand in his, I know all will be well.

He guides me around corners and down walkways until we reach an open building with a glowing orange light at the back. Well-crafted weapons and tools are lined up in a glass window to the right, while unfinished ones sit in piles and racks inside. He enfolds me in the dark, his lips landing on mine, so suddenly I'm reacting when they're gone.

He turns back toward me from the shadows and opens his palm to reveal a tiny ring. It is decorated in crystals and centers a dented chunk of lead as the centerpiece.

"It's for you since it's the part of you that's been closest to my heart."

I don't know what to say, so I hold out my hand and let him slip it onto my finger. No one taught him this because he slid it on my pointer finger with satisfaction. Then, he opens the forge beside us and uses the light of the fire to bring me further into the space.

Conceptually, I knew Kethi did blacksmithing. His mother had mentioned it early after my arrival. Some people in the village said he made their tools for them, but seeing it up close was different. When he was acting as King, that's precisely what it was – acting. Here, he seemed like himself. This was passion.

"I've been working on these," He says, leading me to a row of weapons fashioned after my gun. Tiny teardrop crystals dipped in a transparent casing sit next to them in various sizes. "None of them work yet. But soon enough, they will."

"This is amazing," I tell him honestly, picking up a gun sized almost perfectly for my grip. It's heavier than my own but just as small.

"Some of our women dissected the creature of the abyss and found a soft spot we could shoot for, with these or with our arrows, if they were to come further into Valkarra. If we could get near that spot with one of these, it would have the force to cut through the sack that keeps them alive."

"Tell me about these," I say, replacing the gun in my hand with one of the cased crystals.

"Well, the big issue with your gun is that it injured me, but our *jisa* strengthens from crystals, so even in the case of an accident like ours, this bullet would provide strength to the *jisa* if it were to hit my skin. This bullet could never kill me."

"They could never kill any *V`òllø*." I murmur, understanding and excitement building in my chest.

"Exactly, they would be great for hunting and protecting our people from any threat from the skies. Protect our women as they explore."

"Have you shown anyone else?"

"Liro knows, and I would show them to the Nusosan people."

"They would need to be trained. The *V`òllø* and the Nusosan." I say, a smile growing on my face.

"I thought about that. The weaponry is simple but still dangerous in the wrong hands." He smirks. I put the bullet down as he hooks me onto his lap. "I said to myself, I wonder if my brilliant *ĝha*, who can kill a beast in close contact with her *ĝha*, alone, in the dark, would be willing to help the people learn how to aim such a weapon. I wonder if she would be willing to test my prototypes on long hunts in the forests."

Kethi nuzzles closer to me, placing hot kisses along my neck.

"Your *ĝha* would be interested. A real place among her new people, where she could use all her dusty military training."

He trails kisses to my ear, nipping my earlobe with a fang and tugging gently. Goosebumps skitter down my side as I tilt my head toward his. In the silence of the smithy, my lips met his, and everything felt right.

We didn't have all the answers yet. We didn't know exactly how vital these new weapons would be. But we did know two things for sure. One, we were *ĝhajo* – true mates blessed by some divine power to be together forever. And two, no matter what the future threw at us, we would face it together.

THE END

EPILOGUE
Priscille

Abbess Carlow would have reprimanded me for the thoughts circulating in my mind. Unfortunately, that was nothing new, and Abbess Carlow wasn't here. My parents thought discernment was for me, and that was their first mistake. Obviously, The Big Guy agreed. Why else would he have dumped me on an alien planet?

On the ship, I was meant to stick with the sisters invited to minister in space. My parents believed seeing the universe God created would fix any issues I retained from the first trial of faith. That was their second mistake. Watching the sisters die in service of God did little to help me feel like I was on the right path. This leads me to now - if God did exist, he stuck me with a goddess in triplicate, magical crystals, and indescribable bonds between strangers. How was I supposed to retain my faith now?

I could practically hear Abbess Carlow in my mind. She never yelled in real life, but it was always shouting in my head. Today, it was *Pray! You need to pray more.*

Well, Abbess, I had been praying. I had prayed thrice daily since arrival – since I learned where the holy space was and even before. I had spent more time on my knees in recent days than I did in my entire life as a devout Catholic. And I can't lie; my joints ached, my mind hurt, and I felt no closer to an answer than before hanging around the nuns. If anything, I only began to wonder if God had died in the pod crash with the Old Priscille. I found a temple on Shojo and practically trapped myself in it after Roxie's wedding, trying to determine if going with Serkha was right for me. I took the restlessness in my soul as the indication that I should accompany the *V`òllø* woman.

She was kind to me, answering my questions gently. She asked me questions of her own about Earth and my faith. She invited me onto the ship because she believed The Baso Sheva wanted me there. And she made me feel less of an inconvenience by saying she would like me there too. I had a feeling, which I hoped was God, I would find some answers on the excursion.

That's how I found myself saying goodbye to my closest friend on Shojo. Clara's arms were a vice around me as the winged man, King Solispera, stood behind her. Lanting over her like I was a threat, he kept his eyes on her. He breathed a sigh of relief when she stepped away from me.

"Is this truly what you want to do?" She asked, her hands clenched in her skirts.

If it were anyone else, I would tell them I could feel something out there for me, that God's peace would envelop me when I found it, but this was Clara. We had bonded over our ability to follow blind – her joke, not mine – and became real friends when we decided to go to Valkarra together. Staying with the same host family, learning each other's quirks, and bonding over our shared interest in the new and exciting world we landed on meant leaving her would be hard. So, I admitted my truth. Did I want to do this?

"I'm not sure, but I need to find where I fit in."

Clara gave me another hug with an extra squeeze, resting her head on my shoulder as I hugged her back. It muffled her voice against me, but it was clear when she whispered, "You better bring me back the wildest of stories."

"Always," I promised, even though I had no idea how much I meant it.

ACKNOWLEDGEMENTS

There are many people I would like to thank when it comes to Roxie's Alien Leader, but here are the few who stood out.

First and foremost, I want to throw thanks out there for all the readers who picked up Vera's Alien Leader, and read and reviewed. The support of the series is how I keep it going.

Next, I always have to thank my beta babes. Libby especially this round, with her willingness to provide detailed feedback and deal with all my follow up questions.

I also want to shout out my dogs - Goliath and Ande for cuddling with me through the editing stages and forcing me to take the breaks I need. They'll never read this, but I need everyone else to know that they are pivotal part of the team.

Finally, I want to thank my husband. Truthfully, he is the most valuable player in the MVP circle. Thank you for taking hours out of your evenings to listen to me plot and read and spiral over the feedback I didn't want to hear. Thanks for supporting me in every way.

Last but certainly not least, thank you reader, whether new or old. I hope you enjoyed.

BOOK CLUB DISCUSSION

1. If you have Vera's Alien Leader, you have spent time in Wupeso and Valkarra, which do you prefer? Why?
2. Kethi makes many mistakes in his pursuit of Roxie's love (i.e not telling her they were bonded). How did you feel about the growth they experienced throughout the story? Do you feel like Kethi grew and developed?
3. Roxie's relationship with her new alien family on Valkarra becomes essential to her happiness. Which supporting characters stood out to you, and how did they contribute to the development of the main characters?
4. Throughout the book, Roxie and Kethi face various trials and challenges. Which specific moments or obstacles do you think tested their bond the most, and why?
5. The book delves into the dynamics of power and control, both in personal relationships and political systems. Discuss the instances of power struggles and how they affect the characters' decisions and the overall plot.

Thank you for reading "Vera's Alien Leader"! If you've enjoyed the book and would like to stay connected, here are some ways to do so:

Visit MadisonValePublishing.com

Sign up for our mailing list to receive exclusive content, book recommendations, and notifications about new releases directly in your inbox. Stay in the loop and be among the first to know about any exciting developments.

Follow @madi.vale on Instagram

Consider leaving a review of "Roxie's Alien King" on platforms such as Goodreads, Amazon, or other book review websites.

www.ingramcontent.com/pod-product-compliance
Lightning Source LLC
Chambersburg PA
CBHW072129300726
48975CB00003B/990